ON THE MARKET

THE BALLARD BROTHERS OF DARLING BAY, BOOK 1

RACHAEL HERRON

HGA PUBLISHING

OTHER BOOKS BY RACHAEL

Don't miss a minute in Darling Bay! **One unforgettable town, three standalone series (read them in any order!).** So many ways to fall in love!

THE SONGBIRDS OF DARLING BAY:
  Nashville meets the Gilmore Girls in this heart-warming new trilogy of estranged country-singing sisters seeking true love (and their way back to each other).

The Darling Songbirds, Book 1
The Songbird's Call, Book 2
The Songbird's Home, Book 3

THE FIREFIGHTERS OF DARLING BAY:

Playing with fire has never been this fun...
Blaze: Tox and Grace - Book 1
Burn: Coin and Lexie - Book 2
Flame: Hank and Samantha - Book 3
Heat: Caz and Bonnie - Book 4
Or get all four together on sale, HALF OFF! Save $5.97!
The Firefighters, Boxed Set

THE BALLARD BROTHERS OF DARLING BAY:

The Bachelor meets The Property Brothers: Love,

property, and construction. What could possibly go wrong?

On the Market, Book 1
Build it Strong, Book 2
Rock the Boat, Book 3

STANDALONE NOVELS:

Women and families finding their ways back to what really matters: each other:

The Ones Who Matter Most
Splinters of Light
Pack Up the Moon

CYPRESS HOLLOW ROMANCES 1-5:

Knit-lit with more heat than just wool could ever provide:

How to Knit a Love Song

How to Knit a Heart Back Home
Wishes & Stitches
Cora's Heart
Fiona's Flame
Eliza's Home (Historical Novella)

MEMOIR:

Rachael's life as seen through the sweaters she's knitted:

A Life in Stitches

ON WRITING:

Fast-Draft Your Memoir: Write Your Life Story in 45 Hours

Onward, Writer!

THRILLER (writing as RH Herron)

"Mama, help me." A 911 dispatcher answers the phone, and it's her daughter on the other end of the line.

Stolen Things

COPYRIGHT

ONE

Felicia Turbinado put her rental car into park and glanced back down at the address she'd scribbled on a Post-it. The numbers she'd written matched those on the side of the purple house, yes. So this must be it.

But she'd expected an office-looking building.

This was a dark purple Victorian. And it wasn't a stunning architectural marvel, nothing like the Painted Ladies of San Francisco hours south of here. This place had peeling paint and warped glass in the windows. The small, attached garage seemed to be listing away from the house itself, as if it were trying to slink away without being noticed. The steps that led up to the front door had been dark blue at one point, but footsteps had worn the paint off in the middle of the stair treads. A wind chime hanging from an eave just clunked, its strings tangled.

The sign in front read *Ballard Brothers Building and Realty,* though. It had to be right.

Felicia checked her bag. Contract and deal memo, yes. Signing pen, yep. Non-disclosure agreement, check. Sometimes she carried bribes from her boss with her—Apple watches in 18-Karat gold cases or floor-level season tickets to the closest national basketball team.

But Natasha said this guy was perfect for the new show, and more than that, he wasn't the kind to even know to ask for a bribe. *But just in case, take the big American Express.* Felicia patted the side of her purse as if to reassure herself that with that amount of credit, she could get almost anything done.

Natasha trusted her to close this deal. The brothers would agree to buy a house for a single woman chosen by the network, and then they'd remodel it on camera. Hopefully, attraction would spark between the female buyer and one of the brothers (and the network was willing to pay as much as it took to make that happen).

This was important. Felicia checked her lipstick —the deep red was on her lips and not on her teeth —and her eyeliner was smudged as artfully as she could manage. She got out of the car and gave a sharp tug to her red blouse. This might be a sleepy beach town that smelled of salt and sunscreen, but she was no surfing tourist.

She walked past the rusty old truck in the driveway and went up the stairs. She gave a quick rap at the door.

"It's unlocked, come on in!" The bellow was accompanied by a crash.

Felicia swung the door open.

"I'm in here, to the right!"

The floor was old and dark, and the air smelled of ancient wood polish. To the left was a small office with a cluttered desk that stood in front of windows open to the street.

"Keep going—I'm in the kitchen!"

"Hello?" She peered around a doorjamb.

"Hey there!" The man's back was to her. His hair was short and dark, business-like, and his neck was wide. He turned his head briefly and she caught a glimpse of a broad smile, white teeth. His hands moved rapidly, juggling bread bags and at least three different kinds of jellies. "I just gotta get these sandwiches done."

The house might be old, but inside, it looked classically remodeled. Everything looked vintage and in perfect condition. The refrigerator was lemon-colored. The stove was light orange. A cheerful blond wooden island matched the beveled cabinets. The sheer height of the far windows was astonishing—they let in the view of a massive rear garden. From where Felicia stood in place, her bag pressed to her side, she could see a tangle of tomatoes that looked ready to take over the nearby beanstalks. A long picnic table stood on a low deck, surrounded by heavy outdoor chairs. It looked like a perfect place to hang out. Or to serve a million peanut butter sandwiches, although didn't they have a meeting scheduled? "I'm sorry, did I get the time of our meeting right?"

"Yep, yep, I'm just running a little late, that's all. Let me slap some lids on these bad boys, and we'll get down to business."

"Can I help?" The request was automatic. He'd turn her down, and then they'd have their meeting. She could talk him into the terms of the show, answer all his questions, get his and his brothers' signatures, and be ready to shoot as soon as they found a woman who wanted to buy and remodel a house with these guys.

"Really? Sure. Those all need their crusts cut off. These seven are fine, but Timbo's allergic to peanut butter, so I have to make sure I make his almond butter and strawberry with different utensils. No cross contamination, you know?" He turned to face her.

His eyes were astonishing—a bright, very light blue. Robert Redford eyes. The color of calving icebergs. He had to be wearing contacts. Didn't he? He wore a blue button-down shirt and a darker blue tie, beautifully tied. His shave was smooth, his chest was broad, and his wrists were wide. He looked like a realtor, and a successful one, which is why it didn't make any sense at all that he was working on a production line of sandwiches.

"Felicia, right? I'm Liam. Sorry my hands are too nut-buttery to shake."

"Of course." Smoothly, Felicia swallowed her surprise and set her purse down on the kitchen table. She washed her hands at the sink, and then picked up the knife. "This is more jelly than I've seen since the grade school cafeteria."

"I swear this won't take long. I'm almost done."

Felicia cut off an edge, and then another. It was too bad she hadn't come with a camera crew. How perfect was this? "This was the way I wanted my sandwiches cut when I was a kid."

"I always liked the crusts best myself."

"My mom said that's where the nutrition was."

"Well, no wonder you didn't want to eat them. Nutrition is fine. But not fun."

Felicia liked his voice—it was deep, with a ragged edge. He sounded cheerful, as if he laughed a lot. Maybe he'd actually be likable, a welcome thought. Scouting trips for the network were usually deadly dull—there was a lot of time spent talking with people who had stars in their eyes and no real knowledge about how television worked. They thought that talking to a network rep meant they were guaranteed fame, fortune, and a line of housewares at Target. Felicia had met with women who got plastic surgery just to talk to her. One woman had barely been able to smile around her newly-full lips (they hadn't ended up signing her). There was talented and there was camera-ready, and often they didn't go together.

"Do you live here, too?" It didn't seem like an office kitchen—it seemed like a place a person could cook a holiday turkey or make blueberry pancakes.

"Yep." He glanced at the ceiling. "Upstairs. Okay, I need about six more, then we'll be good."

"Who are we making these for? Do you run an orphanage?" *Please say yes.* Damn, she *should* have brought Tony. Her cameraman would have done a slow pan on the old-fashioned kitchen and then a tight zoom in on Liam's wide hands scraping out the last of the peanut butter. Start the story with his adoration of the children who surrounded him, end with him being in love? The network hadn't managed an Emmy yet, but that might do it.

"You could call it that," he said. "Okay if we deliver these on our way? Won't take long, then we can scout houses. I have a few properties that might work."

"Sure." Heck, yes, she wanted to watch this man deliver sandwiches to whatever lucky group was getting them.

The network might swing and miss at random shows, but Felicia's boss Natasha was rarely wrong. She'd come up with the whole idea while on vacation in the small town of Darling Bay, and it didn't look like she'd be wrong now. With this guy on a show? People would tune in. And the more people who tuned in, the bigger Felicia's bonus would be. Maybe this sleepy little seaside burb would turn out to be all right. No matter what, it had to be better than the show Felicia had just wrapped about a group of sisters trying to break into the soap-making world. If she never had to smell boiling lye again, it'd be too soon.

A NorCal beach town in summer had to be better.

And even though Felicia vastly preferred watching on-screen talent from either the edit room or the comfort of her own sofa at home, it wouldn't be difficult to work with this man with the melting icecap eyes.

TWO

Liam should have expected that the network producer would be pretty. Even though Darling Bay was ten hours north of Los Angeles up the rugged northern California coast, and even though Liam hadn't had cable in years, he knew enough about Hollywood to know that no one was ugly in Tinseltown.

And this woman was stunning. Even in high heels, most women couldn't meet Liam's eyes straight on, but she could, and Liam stood an easy six two. Her dark brown hair was thick and long and curled—it hung to the tops of her breasts, which were round and high and probably fake. She filled out her red shirt perfectly. Her legs were miles long in tapered black pants, and her black heels had to be four inches high. Spikes. Who wore spiked heels in Darling Bay? Cowboy boots and flip flops were the two most popular footwear choices in town, always had been.

He opened his car door. Might as well get this half-baked idea over with so he could get back to the rest of his day. "Here we go. Sorry, I was driving a buyer around yesterday, and I don't think she broke five feet. Just shoot the seat back, that button there."

Felicia nodded and settled into the passenger seat with a long stretch, smooth and graceful. The leather seats gave a sigh like they were happy to meet her.

"Is that okay? You comfy?"

She smiled. "Perfectly."

"Good. Good." His throat felt tight.

Felicia made him nervous.

And that didn't set right with Liam. Yet one more thing that rubbed him wrong about this whole idea.

But he'd be polite about it. If it didn't work, it wasn't a big deal. He'd tell her he couldn't help her. It happened, after all, every once in a while. He'd agree to take a potential client to look at open houses, and on their first trip out, it would be obvious they couldn't work together. The person would be too aggressive or too impatient. Liam liked making money, sure, but he already made enough day to day. He didn't have to take on clients who would be problems from start to finish.

And being on a reality show? Liam's brother Aidan had said it was a stupid idea, but his youngest brother Jake had laughed and called it too weird *not* to look at closer. Liam had been drunk when the idea had come up, and didn't *quite* remember why he'd agreed. So this was on him, really. He'd finish out the meeting with Felicia, show her a couple of houses and prove to her that Darling Bay wasn't the small town they were looking for, and then he'd shake hands politely and vamoose. He'd send a polite email saying thanks but no thanks, that they just didn't have the time. He should have already done that, but this woman's boss, Natasha, had been pushy when she called, and telling a woman she couldn't have what she wanted was his least favorite part of being a realtor.

But the money.

Damn it, with the money Natasha had implied might be in it for them, he and his brothers could start the after-school program for at-risk youth they'd been trying to talk the city into creating for years. They wouldn't have to wait for the city council to agree, they could just do it.

Felicia spoke as if she were interviewing him on camera. "So what makes you good at your job?"

Liam turned right on First Street and gave a

quick wave at Vivian Engel. "Never really thought about it."

"You must have."

"Dunno. I guess I just like to make people happy." After-school program or no after-school program, TV didn't make anyone happy. Liam's gut was right—he knew it. He'd be polite, show her around, and then wave her off into her Hollywood sunset.

Felicia shifted slightly in her seat so that her body faced him more. He caught the scent of her perfume, thick and sweet and rich, like jasmine on a hot night. "Tell me more."

"It's not a big thing. I just know what people are looking for." Aidan called it Liam's superpower. *Me and Jake get 'em all riled up but you calm 'em down, so we almost cancel each other out.* "I can figure out what buyers want before they're really able to verbalize it. And then I just show them those properties."

"So you already know what I'm looking for?"

Her voice was business-like, but it held a sultriness that could earn a woman like her lots of free drinks in dive bars. Nah, on second thought, a woman like Felicia went to intimate, cutting-edge clubs where you had to use a password to get in. She'd probably never set foot in a restaurant with peanut shells on the floor or a bar that smelled like spilled beer.

He pushed the button to roll down the window, suddenly too hot. "Sure I do."

"Tell me." She rolled down her window, too.

Warm summer heat filled the car, and Liam regretted not blasting the air conditioning instead. "Big. Light. Airy. Open plan kitchen, a long redwood deck that overlooks the ocean. Marble and granite floors. Loft bedroom." He glanced sideways at her.

Was that a grimace? "You'd think that, wouldn't you?"

"What?"

"Natasha explained her idea to you, right?"

Liam thumped the gear shaft into second as the pickup in front of him hit its brakes. "Yeah. Sure. Um, did she happen to mention that I was drunk as a skunk that night me and my brothers met her?"

A cool nod. "She did."

"That was only like a month ago. Y'all move this fast?"

"Always."

"I have to say, I *don't* really remember her goal with all this. Some kind of TV show, I know, but Aidan and Jake and me, we're not sure why the hell anyone would want to watch something in a little whistle-stop town like Darling Bay."

"People are tired of glitter." She pointed at Martha's Market. "They want charming. Small town. Warm. Do you know who those people are?"

In front of the store, Parrot Freddy stood with a bird on either shoulder, talking animatedly to Dot Rillo. Freddy had been up in arms since the price of postage stamps went up last summer, and even though Dot only worked at the post office and didn't set the postal rate, Freddy brought it up with her every time he saw her. Dot usually just took the opportunity to try to get Ethel to squawk her classic, *Polly's an idiot, give me a Twinkie.*

"Yeah, I know them."

"See?" Felicia clapped her hands together quickly. "That's what we want. Small-town *The Bachelor* meets *The Property Brothers,* only there are three of you, so that's even better."

"Yeah. Those property guys are kind of creepy, don't you think?"

"Really?" She sounded astonished. "They're handsome twins. People love them."

"They're so *manicured.*" If that's what they were looking for, the Ballard brothers would be right out. Aidan only shaved once a week, maybe twice, and Jake lived on a boat, for cripe's sake. "And they're *actual* twins. It's not like we're triplets or something. We're not that interesting."

"You're Irish triplets, right?"

"Is that even a real thing?" Liam pulled into the driveway at the south end of the high school.

"You're each separated by ten months, right? Like Irish twins?"

"Ten and a half." If you wanted to get technical.

"Your parents were busy."

Yep. That's what everyone said. Predictable as summer fog. "They were also missing in action by the time I was five."

"You're *kidding*."

He glanced at her as he pulled up the parking brake. Had those bright green eyes of hers actually lit up at the thought of them being essentially orphaned?

Television people, man.

"This'll just take a second. You wanna come with me?"

She smiled. "Yes."

That *smile* of hers. That was the kind of smile that launched a thousand ships, or at least the dreams of them. For a reckless moment, Liam imagined saying yes to whatever this woman wanted. "Come on, then."

THREE

The man was a dream. He was everything they'd been looking for. And this was supposedly the non-rugged one? How could that *be?*

They walked along the edge of the parking lot and passed a swimming pool that was surrounded by chain link. Liam's stride was long, and Felicia had to take quick steps to keep up. Blasted heels. What had she been thinking, putting on Louboutins? This wasn't Rodeo Drive, and she knew it.

They passed an empty tennis court, the ground pocked and uneven. The whole school had a run-down vibe, the paint worn off and faded. Seagulls argued at the edge of a dented trash can and pulled at something that looked like a potato chip bag.

Graffiti on the handball wall poked out from under a haphazard application of green paint.

This was *so* not Beverly Hills. The show would want a shabby-chic seaside vibe, but not in a Coney-Island-in-winter way. Hopefully they wouldn't need footage here.

Liam stopped in front of the basketball courts. "This is it."

Once Felicia had gone to the Cinque Terra in Italy to scout a possible vacation reality show. The idea had ended up tanking, and she couldn't even remember the premise for it, but she'd never forgotten the old man she'd met at the water's edge in Vernazza. He'd been impressively short, dressed in an old blue suit. He'd chattered at them about his loves, all of them. *I've had so many loves in my life. And look, here are a few of them.* He'd opened a bag and started setting down kibble right onto the pavement. Dozens of cats—who had been invisible until that moment—appeared from every direction. They ran at him, mewing and crying, and Felicia thought she'd never seen anything sweeter. An old man, surrounded by fifty-plus cats, all of whom loved him (or at least who had loved his treats).

The boys on the basketball court reacted to Liam the same way. Two balls that had been in play bounced by themselves to a stop as they crowded him. The kids seemed to come out of nowhere, more of them every time she looked.

"Quick!" He handed her a heavy paper bag. "Crustless, these ones here. One goes to Timbo—"

"Me!" A boy tall enough to be a man with a face too juvenile to allow him to buy cigarettes raised his hand. He leaped at the sandwich she held out in its plastic bag. "I'll take two! No, can I have three?"

Liam gave her a quick nod. "Jones and Logan get crustless, too."

Quick hands shot out and relieved her of her burden.

"Who else? Jimmy, you like grape, right?"

"Thanks, Liam!"

"Thanks, lady!"

"This is Felicia, say hello..."

But as quickly as they'd arrived, the boys were gone, all of them chewing and jumping and leaping, taking huge bites while simultaneously throwing the retrieved balls at the backboards. Even the cats in Vernazza had taken longer to finish their dinners.

"Okay, that's taken care of."

"Is one of those kids yours?"

Liam balled up his paper bag and shot it at the trash can, making it easily. His fist pumped. "Two points! You ready?"

Felicia blinked. Liam was easy on the eyes, all

right. He'd be great in front of the camera. His smile was wide, his teeth white and straight. Even though he was ostensibly the paper-pusher of the brothers, it was obvious that his blue button-down shirt hid a muscular chest and a flat stomach.

She needed to stop staring. "Yeah."

Back in the car, Liam was more talkative, as if the brief visit with the boys had relaxed him a bit. She hadn't noticed he was nervous—and most regular people were, talking to networks reps—but he must have been.

Now, though, he'd loosened his tie a notch. His elbow stuck out the open window as he narrated their drive. "Down there is the main fire station. See, where the flagpole is? They're about to do their boot drive, and that'll be fun."

"Boot drive?"

"Once a year, they stand at every intersection in town holding a uniform boot, and people throw money at them. For every balled-up dollar bill that lands in the boot, they have to do a quick dance."

"Is that a punishment for something?"

"You kidding? Those guys love to show off. Two of them know how to break dance. They put those guys at the stoplight."

"*The* stoplight? Singular?"

"We just need one."

"Wow." Felicia did a calculation in her head. "When does this happen?"

Liam's smile faded a little. "Why? You want to get that on camera or something?"

"I have to tell you, Darling Bay seems almost too good to be true. We want stories, and everything you say seems to be the start of a good one."

"Well." Liam turned his head, and Felicia couldn't see his expression. "Let me show you the properties I had in mind before you get too excited."

"I don't get too excited."

"Oh, really?" He sounded amused.

"Unflappable." She wouldn't admit that she was feeling more hopeful than she normally did on scouting trip.

"Is that as fun as it sounds?"

"Less," she admitted.

FOUR

The first house should send her running, although Liam personally loved it.

It was a clumsy seventies build, twenty-two hundred square feet of awkward space. The rooms were small and poorly painted, but the structure seemed solid, and the termite report was clear. It was on a quiet residential street, and from the master bedroom balcony a person could *just* see a glimpse of the marina if he leaned the right way.

"Water view, excellent." Felicia checked something off from her list and snapped a photo with her cell phone.

"As you can see, it's a little dated, but it's move-in ready." Liam closed the sliding-glass door and a small black piece of its handle dropped to the ground. "Whoops."

Felicia cleared her throat and tapped her pencil on her clipboard. "How much did Natasha tell you about the concept of the show?"

"You bring us an interested buyer. We find them a house at the high end of their price range, I haggle the seller down, and then my brothers fix it up." Liam would be the guy wearing the suit, not the tool belt. As usual. It was too bad he couldn't hammer a nail without driving it through his thumb.

"That's *kind* of close..."

"Wait. So that's the Property Brothers part." Liam clicked the plastic piece back into place where it belonged on the cheap handle. "What was that part you said about *The Bachelor?*"

Felicia smiled, but something in her jaw was tight. "You've seen the show, I'm assuming?"

He led her back into the living room. The pink fireplace was so egregious it hurt his soul. "Nah. Not my style. But I've got a pretty good idea what it's about. Thirty women, one guy? Not bad odds, I guess."

"Right. Well, this would be different."

The show was about love, right? Ostensibly. Having never seen an episode, Liam couldn't be totally certain, but he was pretty sure it was more about lust and looks and backbiting gossip. It was about who could attract a man the fastest.

How did you mix that with a show about selling and fixing up a house?

But hell, he didn't actually care that much. That Natasha boss-woman had roped him into showing these properties, and he'd been mildly curious, but the more he thought about being on camera the more he didn't like it. And Liam didn't want to be inside this house that smelled like oven cleaner and damp carpet much longer. "You've seen enough?"

"I have. I'll send my boss the pictures as we drive."

The next property was close enough that they could have walked, but he didn't mention that to her. Liam wanted his car close by, in case he needed to haul them back in a hurry.

Felicia was tense, too. He could feel it coming off her gorgeous, light brown skin. Then he banished the thought and pressed the accelerator harder. The sooner they got this over with, the sooner he could tell her they were out. The Ballard Brothers were not for sale.

She leaned forward as he slowed. "Is this the next one?"

"Yep. Property number two."

It was a newer home with wide wooden floors

and big picture windows. The bedrooms would need redoing—a buyer could combine the two small ones into a room big enough for a master bedroom or even a double office. The neighborhood was great, and while there was no ocean view, there was a small hill on the back of the property that held an old orchard. Who could resist homegrown apricots in summer and apples in fall?

"Can't wait to see it." She gave him that rapid smile again, the one that made Liam feel like he was a little off balance.

"You'll love the backyard."

But Felicia barely looked at the place. True, she nodded in all the right places, and she made notes on her clipboard, but she wasn't paying attention to the words he was reeling off at her.

And that was fair. Liam wasn't really thinking about them either. He led her outside and showed her the ripe strawberries.

"That one's a peach tree, I think." Liam pointed at the tree which was covered in avocados.

"Mmm." She took a photo of it. "Great."

Okay. He didn't really *care* about the show, since they weren't going to do it, but he wanted to know. Liam turned to face her. Over her head, a small plane rose from the local airport and climbed into the bright blue sky. "What's with *The Bachelor* thing?"

Felicia didn't glance up from her paperwork. "Sorry?"

"Tell me. I can't figure it out."

Felicia didn't meet his gaze. Instead, she looked up at the plane. "It's no big deal. You help an eligible woman buy a house and fix it up. Hopefully one of you falls in love with her."

"*What?*" Liam took a step backward.

"You're under no obligation, of course."

"To fall in *love?*"

Felicia pulled a glasses case out of her bag and pushed black sunglasses onto her face. "Bright out here."

"That's insane. That's the premise?"

"I believe Natasha said you came up with it."

"No way." Oh, god. A memory as skinny as a dime filtered to the surface—him, drunk as a skunk's uncle in The Golden Spike, roaring with laughter at what the big city television producer was going on about. Something about finding love in the sticks. "She told you I was drunk?"

"Yeah."

"She told you why?"

"Something about getting dumped?"

"That's a polite word for it, yeah. Jilted."

Felicia pushed her sunglasses farther up her nose. "So it was recent?"

"Nah, a year ago. More now. My brothers and I

were celebrating a year of me being single. Kind of like a reverse anniversary."

"Was it at the altar? That she jilted you?"

"Night before." He'd called Brandy to see why she was late to the rehearsal dinner. She'd sent a text. *Wedding's off. I thought you were the right guy, but I was wrong. Sorry.*

And the funny part was that *he* was the one who hadn't quite felt ready to get married.

"That must have been hard." She looked down at her feet and shifted her weight. "Anyway, Natasha was just glad she met you all that night. She loved each one of you."

"Even Jake?"

Felicia smiled. "The fisherman, right? Even Jake. She came up with the property angle, but she said you were the one who came up with the love angle. That's what sold her."

"Yeah, see, the bar has this signature drink called a Golden Spike. Two of those and you think you can fly to the moon on your bicycle. I think Dixie made me six of them. That I remember. I would have agreed to marry an orangutan."

"You're lucky that didn't occur to you."

"Are we sure it didn't?"

That same smile flashed across her face again. It was so pretty, but there was a tightness at the corners of her mouth. What did it take to get her to really cut loose and laugh? "She didn't mention anything like that. She just said that the three of you are bachelors, and that you all look alike." Felicia slid her glasses down a moment and looked him from head to toe. "Do you?"

"Well, yeah. And I'm the handsome one."

Her lips twitched. He was getting closer. "Ah."

"I still don't get it. So what, like *The Dating Game?*"

"Natasha would hate you to think her glossy show would be anything like a seventies game show, but maybe you're right. The network would pick a woman we like. She'll be someone who's looking for a home to buy, a woman starting her life over in a new place. She's probably independently employed, with enough money but not overly wealthy."

"Or else why would she play?"

Her voice was dry. "Exactly. The three of you help her find and fix up the house of her dreams. And in the meantime, the network pays for extravagant dates, should any of you decide that would be fun."

"Fun." This was getting more and more bizarre. "What's extravagant mean to you?"

"You'd make that call, but I can imagine something like while the house gets a new kitchen installed, you and she fly to Paris for two nights. Or if it's Aidan who's hitting it off with her, they go to Venice while you're working on securing the loan and talking the seller down in price. Jake—sorry— what does he do again? Natasha was a bit unclear. You're the realtor and Aidan's the builder, but Jake?"

"Who knows?" Liam's little brother Jake fished. He built boats. He took long naps. Sometimes he helped them with whatever it was they needed—he wasn't bad with an Excel spreadsheet, and he was ace with roof repair. "He helps."

"Fine. And just to confirm—you're all single."

"For the moment. Aidan will probably have a girlfriend by the end of the week and then another one by the week after that."

Felicia jotted something down. "So he's the player?"

"Oh, yeah."

"And Jake?"

"He gets serious about girls and then they break his heart."

"Like you."

Sometimes Liam wished his heart really *had* been broken by Brandy instead of just sucker-punched and insulted. "I guess."

"And you're all straight?"

He felt his eyebrows fly upward. "Sorry?"

"We're thinking of calling it *On the Market.* Do you like it?"

"We're straight but—"

"Not that it would be a real problem. Our audience doesn't mind same-sex couples, and if they do, we don't really care. And actually, a coming-out story would be great if we could pull it off—"

"Good to know that you're progressive." He couldn't keep the sarcasm out of his voice.

"I apologize for having to ask."

Liam wished she weren't wearing those glasses. He really wanted to see her whole face. "Our stepdad was gay, and he was the best man we ever knew."

She gave a brief nod. "You have to know that if we go ahead with this, you'll be subject to a lot of scrutiny. A lot of people will have opinions about your lives, and you'll be able to do nothing to change any of it. At all."

"So why the hell would we be interested in doing this?" If it had any potential at all to hurt his brothers, Liam was even less interested than before. The money would have been nice, but was it really enough? To risk any kind of pain to the people he loved? He should drive her back to her car right now. This was a waste of both their time.

Felicia pointed out the side gate. "Can we get to

the next place? This isn't interesting to me. Avocado tree aside."

She *had* been paying a bit of attention, then. "You didn't answer my question."

She nodded briskly. "The figure Natasha mentioned to you and your brothers?"

The figure that had made Aidan's jaw drop, the sum that had made Jake hoot like a monkey? "Yeah?"

"Ask for double." She walked past him, her stride long and confident. Over her shoulder, she said, "And don't ever tell her I said that."

FIVE

Why did she even just *say* that? Felicia ate, slept and breathed the network. When she saved them money, she felt more satisfaction than she did when she got a bonus. Confessing how much the network would actually pay was something she'd normally *never* do. But something about Liam Ballard threw Felicia so far off her game she wasn't sure what they were playing.

Why the hell had she told him to ask for double?

The brothers would get the price if they asked for it, she knew that. This town was as darling as its twee name, and if Liam's brothers really did look anything like him, the show would be solid gold. Liam was built like a mountain climber—no, more like a Scottish highlander. She could imagine him striding the summit in a kilt, letting the wind blow where it may. Liam was hot as hell, wide and tall and rangy with those light blue eyes that reminded her of summer mornings and faded denim. And he was the money guy, the one who was more pocket-protector than tool belt. Natasha said the other two brothers were even more rugged.

Gold.

And if you added the element of potential love and attraction? The Ballard Brothers starring in *On the Market* would be the hit of the year. The men could literally name their price.

Felicia needed to pull herself together. Sure, she fell halfway in love with every male reality show star she'd ever put in front of a camera. It was the same kind of love she felt for the guys on *The Vampire Diaries* or *Jessica Jones*—they were all comfortably far enough away to be enjoyable with the added bonus of being click-off-able with her remote control.

She was scouting. She was putting together the package, making it something the network would salivate over while at the same time making the primary players feel like it was too good to be true (and it usually was—no one expected how much their lives would change from being a household name).

Felicia Turbinado came in and got the job done. Emotions didn't come into it.

So it was just plain weird that she felt nervous. Why? It couldn't be just sitting next to this Liam. Hollywood was packed with hot men. Her pool guy had cheekbones that would make Michelangelo weep.

Maybe she was just tired. She wanted to close the deal, make it back to her bed and breakfast, and call it a day.

Surreptitiously, Felicia watched Liam's legs as he drove. It was a fancy car—leather seats and dual climate control and Wi-Fi—he'd chosen it to make clients comfortable as he drove them around. But he'd bought a manual transmission as if he didn't need to make things easy for himself. He sat far from the wheel, holding it with one hand, and his left leg flexed as he shifted. His nails were short and not buffed. Felicia would bet her last dollar he didn't shave his chest like most of the men she knew in Southern California. Poor guys—they'd gotten off so easy for so long in the grooming department. That was all different now. But Felicia herself preferred a natural guy, one who went scruffy on the weekends, one who smelled like himself after a day's work.

"Do you ever help your brothers with construction?"

Liam snorted. "No."

"Why not?"

"Maybe they're threatened by me?" He waved at yet another person he appeared to know.

"Really?" That would play well on screen.

He shot her a sideways look. "I was joking. Sadly, I'm better with the wood in a pencil than a two by four. Look, this is the last place on my list." Liam pulled down a long dirt driveway, rutted but wide. "This probably won't be the right one. A lot of people would call this eccentric, but it was the last one I had in your price range."

The network's lowball range, that was. Felicia knew they could go higher, but that wasn't the point of this show. They weren't looking for a mansion to redecorate. They wanted a moderate house in a nice neighborhood, somewhere around half a million—something upwardly middle income viewers could aspire to, if not actually afford. Something a bit shabby perhaps that could be refreshed and modernized. *Open planned.* Felicia hated that phrase already, and the show hadn't even gone into production yet. Knocking out walls and making great rooms out of small ones—that was all anyone talked about. When she'd bought her condo three years before, it had been hard to find anything that wasn't work/live loft space. Light and air, she got it. And sure, for the network, it was all about the footage. A small room looked even tinier when it was on television. But for *real* living, what about smaller rooms? Cozy ones, full of loved furniture and books and paintings? What was wrong with those?

Liam took the final potholed turn. "But even eccentric, it's kind of a beaut, you have to admit."

Felicia leaned forward, her mouth falling open. This was a house? That was for *sale?* "I can't—what is going on here?"

The house was a faded gray two-storied ramshackle place, with a wraparound porch, but that wasn't what made her heart race.

There was an enormous tree. Growing right up through the middle of the house.

Felicia's mouth felt dry. This was impossible.

She knew this house.

She'd dreamed about it when she was small. She'd been dreaming about this house for most of her life.

This house.

SIX

She must have seen a picture of it. That was the answer. Maybe the house had been on the cover of *Sunset Magazine* when she was a kid or something. And she'd dreamed about it, and she'd told her mother, and they'd spun whole stories about it. "Oh, my god."

"I know. It's something."

Felicia was halfway out of her seat belt even before Liam came to a full stop. "Is that *real?* The tree?"

"Yep. Redwood."

It was her favorite tree, and this one was huge. It must be two hundred years old, at least. "It's *inside.* The tree is inside the house." She walked quickly toward the house. *This can't be.*

Liam caught up to her, his steps quick in the dirt. "Don't get too excited until you see the inside. It's been vacant a long time."

"I know this house."

"Sorry?"

Felicia was being ridiculous. "It looks like the house grew up around the tree." She stopped in her tracks in order to gaze at it longer, before she got too close and discovered its flaws, before she discovered nothing could possibly be as perfect as this magical dwelling that she'd never known was real.

"Well, you could argue it did."

"Who built it?"

"A man named Henry Maupin, back in the thirties."

Felicia resisted stretching out her hands—she wanted to pluck the house from the air in front of her before it disappeared. "So long ago? But the tree's been growing that whole time, right?"

"It was big then. It's gotten a few feet bigger in diameter, but he allowed for that."

"I can't believe it's for *sale*." How did a dream go on the market? How did someone list a fantasy?

Liam pointed. "Check out the view. I'll go unlock."

Felicia turned.

The ocean.

She gave a sigh that felt as if it scraped the

bottom of her soul. They were far enough up the steep driveway that she could see over the low cypress trees that lined that path. And there it was. The sea.

Water was often said to sparkle like diamonds, but that was so prosaic and inaccurate—*this* water was lit with a rainbow of sparks. Emerald, amethyst, and even hints of ruby glinted as the ocean swells rolled in the sun a mile away. The air smelled of sun and dirt and clean, fresh wind.

A hawk cried from his perch on a power line and two swallows danced past him in the breeze.

This was all *real?*

Felicia turned back to see if the apparition of the perfect house had vanished yet.

Liam stood on the doorstep. He held out a key. "Want to go in?"

"Yes. Yes, yes, yes, *yes*. Yes, I do." She was glad Natasha wasn't there to see her—the unflappable Felicia felt very flapped, indeed.

Yes. She wanted to go in.

The door was short, rounded at the top, as if they were entering a hobbit home. Both of them had to duck to enter. Inside, the room opened into a kitchen with tall, dark wood ceilings. Built-in cabinets lined two of the walls and still held dusty glassware. The air smelled faintly of toast, as if someone had just walked out of the room, plate in hand.

"You said it's vacant?"

"Hasn't been occupied for years."

"Why?"

"The builder's daughter went into a care home a while back. She wouldn't sell it while she was alive, just in case she could ever get back. She died before she could."

Felicia ran her hand along the counter top made of old brown tile. Serviceable. And in this house, magical. "How terrible." To have had to leave this place behind, to know it was there and not be able to be inside it.

The stove stood a foot away from the wall, as if someone had pulled it out to work on it and never got around to finishing. There was just a hole where the refrigerator used to be.

"It needs a lot of work. But wait till you see upstairs."

Felicia let out a whoosh of breath. "Yes, yes, let's go see. Before it all vaporizes into the mist or something."

"It's a three-one fully-furnished farm house priced undervalue because nothing's been retro-fitted. It's not Brigadoon."

One of her very favorite movies. But she didn't say it—she just followed him farther into the house.

The parlor—because Felicia couldn't call it a living room—was perfect, its furniture worn and dusty. Chairs and tiny tables stood in clumps, as if a party of people playing cards had just stepped outside for a moment. The windows were small, and the red velvet curtains were heavy, giving the room a quiet, still feeling. "It needs light."

"Could knock out that back—"

"Don't you *dare* say knock out that wall. It just needs sheer curtains." Felicia undid the latch on one of the casement windows and banged on it with her palm until it screeched open. "And air. There, isn't that better? Oh, my god, look at the *rug*." It was as deep red as the old curtains, and as she looked at it through chair and table legs, she could just make out a stag hunting scene. A woven dog panted on the floor at her feet, and she wanted to step sideways, to preserve the weft. "That's incredible."

Liam's expression was unreadable—were his eyebrows drawn together because he was trying to see what she did or because he was trying not laugh at her? "It's worn through in about seventy-two places."

"It can be fixed. Rugs *can* be fixed, right?" Felicia had no idea, but it was suddenly imperative that it be true.

"I'm sure they can."

"More." She clasped her hands in front of her, scared that she would try to scoop up the whole room and fit everything into her bag. "I want to see more."

"This way, then." Liam gestured to the far door.

They went through the small hallway and into a bedroom that was decorated the same way the parlor had been, with strong, dark furniture that looked sturdy enough to make it into the next century or two. A green coverlet embroidered with darker green French knots was rumpled at the edge, as if someone had sat on it shortly after making it. A hand mirror rested upside down on a vanity, and Felicia barely resisted the urge to turn it over, to look into it, to see if she looked different. "If this has been vacant, how has it not been vandalized? How is it in such good shape?"

"You think *this* is good shape? Where are you from again?"

She swept her arm toward the walls, where deep red floral wallpaper peeled away from the plaster. "No graffiti. Furniture still in place. No one's stolen that mirror."

"This is a small town."

"What about teens?" She'd been to small towns. Kids were kids everywhere. They smoked in dark corners and had unprotected sex on unprotected beds, like the one in this room.

"Well, the kids I know wouldn't do that to a

house the whole town loves. And I know all of them, you might have noticed."

Felicia raised an eyebrow.

"Okay." He held up his hands. "Also, there's an alarm."

"I knew it. Okay. This won't make sense, and I don't expect you to believe me. But I feel like I know this place."

"You've been here before?"

"I'm pretty sure I haven't." She'd never been this far north in California in her life. "But I recognize it. Somehow…"

"Some kind of weird déjà vu? Come take a look at the only bathroom and see if you recognize it. It could use some work, but maybe you already knew that?" His face had relaxed, and his voice held the trace of a laugh.

This feeling was silly. So unlike her. She felt like laughing at herself, too.

She left the bedroom. The hall was narrow, and Liam's shoulders were broad. Her hip brushed his as she entered the bathroom, and she felt a touch of dizziness. The house was getting to her. What else would explain the sudden and completely irrational urge to rest against Liam's chest for a moment while she got her bearings?

The house was playing with her.

And damn, he was right about the bathroom.

The clawfoot tub had rusted all the way through. It wouldn't be salvageable. The pedestal sink was cracked. The floor's broken tiles slanted to one side, and the one small window hung crookedly, a broken tooth in the wall. "Oh."

"Nothing's perfect, right?"

"No." He was wrong. "This house is *everything.* Even with this."

He laughed. "You're delightful."

Felicia blinked. She'd been called many things at the network: speedy, ballsy, thorough, driven. But never delightful. She wasn't even sure if she should take it as a compliment. "Hmm."

"Now, what next?" The smile lingered at the creases at the corners of his eyes.

Felicia's heart race increased. "The tree?" There was a redwood *inside* this house, and she couldn't wait any longer.

"Stairs." He pointed to the far end of the hallway.

The staircase was odd. The steps themselves were normal—average height and depth, covered with a threadbare runner that was tacked to the wood. But instead of just one handrail, it had two, one on either side. The right side dropped into a dining room occupied by a table and ornately carved wooden chairs. The left side of the stair rail, though—it stood four inches away from a rough wooden wall.

She reached out to touch it. "*Oh*. It's the tree."

It was incredible. The trunk was an inner *wall* of the house. Felicia's throat constricted and again she felt that strange urge to laugh out loud.

Liam followed her up, moving slower than she did, which was good. She wanted to be upstairs by herself for just a moment.

The tree stood right smack in the middle of the building.

The room—because it was really only one long room that ran in a wide square around the porch— was bright from inset skylights and surrounded by windows. The whole top floor was one open space. If *this* was what people were going for when they said they wanted open plan construction, well, Felicia could understand that. It was like an enormous cupola, perhaps eight-hundred square feet. The place where the tree pushed out the top of the roof was covered by a dirty canvas tarp.

Liam came up behind her. "That leaks."

"Of course it does. I bet the old girl loves that, when the water drips down to her roots."

"Are you sure you've never been here before?"

"Never." Felicia held up her hand, palm out. "I swear. Why?"

"Mrs. Maupin called the tree the old girl.

You're kind of freaking me out." Liam pushed his hand through his carefully combed hair. Dark locks fell over his forehead—the darkness accentuated his light blue eyes.

Felicia felt a hitch in her chest. "I'm sorry. I must have seen it on TV or a magazine or something when I was a kid. But I feel like I know this place better than anyplace else. My mom and I—" Oh, it was so stupid. She couldn't possibly say it out loud.

But Liam was listening. He nodded and his face was open and friendly, his light blue eyes trained on hers.

As if he really cared what she said next.

"My mom and I had this kind of storytelling game. We lived in a small apartment in Reseda—the best she could afford, but that wasn't much. She worked long hours at an appliance store. She was the night manager." Felicia suddenly remembered how proud she'd been, at ten, when her mother had been promoted, and then at sixteen, how that same job title had embarrassed her so much. A night manager. Her friends' parents had been show runners and directors and even some actors. Her mother sold refurbished vacuum cleaners and washing machines. "So she usually wouldn't get home till after midnight. But I've always been a night owl, and when she'd catch me still awake, she'd have me tell her the stories I made up about our tree house."

"This house."

"Oh, god, it's too weird, I know. Just some gigantic coincidence." Felicia looked up the tree to the canvas tarp. "But if that comes off—if you can climb up there—"

Liam walked to the far side of the truck, his footfall echoing on the wooden boards. "Like this?" He pointed to something she couldn't see.

She came around to him.

A crude ladder of nailed two-by-fours ran up the trunk.

She looked up again. Her stomach fluttered frantically. "How does the tarp come off?" He reached to help, but she was faster. She tugged at a frayed rope that was wrapped around a thick hook. With three pulls, the tarp-covered hole was open so that she could look up through the hole and see the tree climbing into the blue sky.

And above, built into the wide branches that had to be more than fifteen feet in diameter, stood a platform.

"The treehouse that's above the treehouse." The one she'd known would be there.

This was literally the house she and her mother had built in their minds.

Liam spoke from behind her. "Go on up."

"I haven't climbed a tree since...it must have been third grade." Her mother had had a brief stint of believing that Felicia being a latch-key kid wasn't good for her, and she'd gone to play with friends after school rather than reading and watching TV all afternoon, every afternoon. Jennifer Wasatch's dad had built a tree house in the backyard, but it had been rickety and poorly built. The one time they'd gone up intending to start a secret club, Felicia had lost her balance on a wobbly board and torn her foot open on an exposed nail.

"It's safe."

"Really?"

He smiled and tiny creases formed at the corners of his eyes. "It's held a lot more than just little old you."

Little old her. She was almost six feet tall. She hadn't felt little since her seventh-grade growth spurt. She grinned back at him. "Okay."

"You might want to—"

"I know." She kicked off her heels and put her foot on the lowest rung. Grateful she wasn't in a skirt, she climbed up and through the hole at the top and onto the platform.

If she'd tried to tell to someone how it felt to be on top of the entire world, this would be what she described. She could see Liam when she peered over the edge. He stood, looking easy in his skin, his back pressed to the wall. He gave her a lazy thumb's up.

Carefully, she stood. She planted her feet firmly on the wood and felt something grown inside her, as if she herself were growing roots, invisible ones.

The platform was maybe eight feet wide in diameter, with a slight lip all around. When Felicia imagined a tree house, she pictured a box with walls, which—really—was the dumbest thing ever. If you were in a tree, you wanted to be *in a tree.*

Which she was. Firmly. Totally. Up a tree.

Through the branches, she could see over the rooftop down to the marina. The boats looked like toys. An inch of fog had slid up the very edge of the horizon. She caught the scent of dusty leaves, and something greener, more riparian.

Above her, something scrabbled. She jumped. A squirrel—a big, fat, fluffy one—looked down at her and chattered in surprise. "Don't mind me," she said. "I'm just here for a minute."

Felicia wanted the words to be untrue.

She crossed her legs and sat. She wanted to meditate. Or do yoga, using the trunk for stability. Or have a picnic. Anything, not to leave this place. She took a deep breath in and held it as long as she could, trying to memorize the way the sharp leaves sounded as they scraped against each other in the breeze.

"Stay up there as long as you want," Liam called.

"That would be forever."

"That's fine. Should I call your boss and tell her you quit?"

Natasha.

Lord. She'd love something like this for the show. A true challenge.

"I'm coming down." She stretched out her legs and considered not sending Natasha pictures of the aerie. *Don't be ridiculous.* She snapped three and sent them before she could change her mind.

Back down the ladder, inside the main room that made up the second floor, Felicia stood at the window that faced due west, staring at the water far below. "This is insane," she murmured. "Completely insane." She took another photo of the way the trunk of the tree went right up through the roof and hit send.

"Amazing, right? When Mrs. Maupin still lived here, she had her bed up here, instead of the bedrooms downstairs. It's a problem that the one and only bathroom is downstairs, but with a big remodel, there might be enough room to partition this and build one up here."

He sounded like a realtor, but there was something more in his voice. Felicia turned to look at him. His hand rested on the tree trunk and his gaze was soft. He saw it, too. The enchantment of it.

"It's perfect."

"For the show?"

God.

The unsaid words rang in her head: *For me. This is perfect for me.*

SEVEN

An hour later, Felicia was back at the Cat's Meow, the only bed and breakfast in Darling Bay. It was Felicia's worst nightmare when it came to lodging— the entire place was filled with stuffed cats and a surprising number of stuffed sheep, most of which made noises (terrible, mechanical wails and *baaaa*s) if she happened to brush against one, which seemed completely inevitable. The lobby smelled like strawberry jelly, and the scent continued, like bad theme music, into her small room. She wouldn't have stayed if there had been a single other place in town, but apparently the one and only hotel was under construction. The crew, if they did the show, would have to stay a few miles down the coast.

There wasn't even a television, and while in the

past that had been a deal-breaker for her, it did have Wi-Fi, which meant she could still watch her shows on her iPad.

Felicia was good at making television shows because she loved watching them. All of them. Escaping into fantasy had been her favorite part of growing up (watching alone while her mother was at work, lying on her stomach on the orange shag rug), and escaping into fantasy was her favorite part of the job now. Sure, when she wasn't on the road for work, she had friends and a social life, but her favorite thing was still television. The world had gotten easier to navigate when it became possible to watch TV wherever she had an internet connection.

When Felicia had checked in, the strawberry-scented innkeeper had insisted the Wi-Fi was fast. "Yes, dear, I play *lots* of solitaire games on the AOL Google thing, and it just zips along. The password is *password* but please don't share that with anyone."

The balcony of the room made the bed and breakfast almost bearable. It didn't have a great view—only her white rental car and the low-slung blue house across the street were visible—but it was close enough to the water that she could hear the gulls' cries and the boats' low horns. The fog that had been threatening to roll in earlier now cloaked her in damp and drifted down the darkening street like something out of a crime novel. The air was chilly, but pleasantly un-strawberry scented. An old man walking a dog the approximate size of a small horse waved up at her, and she waved back.

That was what they did in this town. They waved at each other.

In LA, you only got waved at with a middle finger.

The Maupin house.

There were one million reasons she couldn't have it, first and foremost being she wasn't in the market for a house. She'd been saving for one, yes. She had a condo, which was a fine place to sleep in. It was well appointed with bland furnishings that she'd always meant to personalize and close enough to work that the commute wasn't usually longer than an hour.

But she lived there. Ten hours south. Her job was in LA. Her friends were there. Her whole *life.*

Tension knotted in her stomach and she leaned forward, pressing her forehead against the cold iron railing.

She couldn't buy a house in Northern California, no matter how much it matched the house of her dreams. And she *especially* couldn't buy a house that her network would probably want to purchase for the show. Before Liam had driven her back to her car, she'd taken more photos of the tree-house and responsibly sent them to Natasha. She'd asked sensible questions about the plumbing and insulation.

Felicia lived in LA.

For the last three shows she'd done for the net-work, she'd seen more of Natasha than anyone else. Natasha was great. Domineering, loud, and whip-smart, Natasha was a good boss. But she wasn't re-ally what Felicia would call a friend.

When was the last time Felicia had gone to book group with the girls? Since *Orphan Train?* Could it be that long? When was the last time she'd gone dancing with Ruby? Or out to any dinner that wasn't work related? When was the last time she'd been on a date that was even the slightest bit in-teresting?

The image of Liam's face—so open and serious —as she told him about her and her mother's tree-house game flashed into her mind. He'd said he was single but did that mean just not-married? Plenty of people were in serious long-term relationships without being married.

Soon, if this show got the green light, Felicia would be going through applications of women wanting to be the one to buy the house Liam was selling, the one who dated him or one of his brothers as her house was remodeled.

What if the unknown beautiful woman—of course she'd be beautiful, no point to the show otherwise—what if she scored both Liam *and* Felicia's house of dreams?

What about that idea made her feel so uneasy, exactly?

Felicia had to get her head on straight. She'd go through some work email. Maybe that would help.

Damn it. She'd left her computer bag on the backseat of the car. Felicia blinked in surprise—she really *was* far from home. In LA, she didn't leave her computer unattended in the car for even a moment. But this was Darling Bay, where boys like the one she was staring at right now—a huge hulk of a kid wearing a red sweatshirt and riding a black bicycle with knobby tires—didn't commit crime, if Liam was right about that. Two more boys followed him, whooping as they caught air on a speed bump. She'd go get the bag now, as soon as they rode away.

As Felicia watched, though, the bigger kid slowed down at her rental car. He peered in the driver's window. He looked up and down the street in all directions but up at her. He tugged at his red baseball cap, pulling it lower, and he straightened the glasses on his face.

Then, at the encouragement of his bike-riding hoodlum friends, he took a carton of eggs out of his backpack and threw an egg at her car. The other boys cheered. The kid threw two more eggs at her windshield, and then he took careful aim at the stop sign she was parked in front of. The egg smacked the metal with a loud *ping*. He tossed four or five more eggs at a mailbox and two at his friends who ducked and laughed.

Liam knew nothing about teens.

Whatever. It was just eggs, and the car was a rental. She'd pull it through a drive through car wash, if this town had one.

But then the kid pulled out what looked like a big Sharpie, and started drawing a fat black line on the passenger door.

Felicia jumped to standing and yelled as loudly as she could, "Hey! Jackass!"

The boy looked up, then he jammed his glasses further up his face. He added one more line and a couple of quickly sketched curves and then threw his bag over his shoulder. All three boys rode furiously up the street as the fog thickened. Their laughter filtered thinly back to her.

Felicia's feet thumped on the rose-covered carpets as she ran downstairs. Pearl Hawthorne, the overeager innkeeper, gave a nervous squeak as she raced past.

It was too late. By the time she got out onto the street, the boys were gone.

Idiots.

"Is everything okay?" Pearl held a stuffed white lamb at her midsection, as if she could use it to protect herself.

Felicia pointed at the penis—quite a good penis, truth be told—on the side of the rental. "Vandalism. I'll have to make a report."

"Oh, dear." Pearl tucked the lamb under her arm and tilted her head to look at the drawing. "Is that supposed to be...a..."

Felicia sighed. "Yeah. A big one. Wishful thinking starts early, I guess."

EIGHT

From his car, Liam texted Aidan. *Meet at Jake's boat.*

I have a date tonight.

The TV deal is real and more $ than we thought. We have to decide. Take your booty call later.

Aidan pulled up at almost the same time Liam did.

"It's not a booty call," Aidan said.

"Yeah?" Liam checked the time on his phone. "You're not *on* a date, and it's already seven. What time does this date start?"

"At midnight, when she gets off work."

"That's a booty call."

"The best *kind* of date." Aidan punched Liam on the shoulder.

"Ow. Dumbass." He rubbed his arm.

"Just 'cause you're a freaking baby—hey, I need to come by to borrow Bill's truck." Aidan winked. "You know how the stars look from that old truck bed…"

"Bill would be horrified by the number of times you get away with that."

"Well, yeah. But then he would laugh."

"Jake! We're coming on board." Liam yelled at the direction of the door that went below deck. Jake was friendly enough, but he owned a gun and didn't mind showing it off when he thought someone might be breaking and entering his sovereign domain. "We have beer!"

The boat was old, but Jake had loved her into the right shape a long time ago. The top deck was a makeshift patio, decorated with old glass fishing floats and strings of red lights in the shape of Chinese lanterns. Liam had spent too many nights to count on this deck, looking up at the stars of Darling Bay with his brothers.

Jake came up on deck, fast. "I was *just* imagining a beer. Do you have pizza, too?"

Liam shook his head. "You wish."

"Damn it."

Aidan peered through the open door. "Whatcha got to eat down there?"

"Bag of stale pretzels."

Aidan nodded. "It'll do."

They sat where they always did: Liam in one of the wooden Adirondack chairs Jake had made from driftwood, Jake in the camping chair with his legs kicked up on a coil of heavy rope, and Aidan on top of the old fish cooler. They clinked bottles and crunched pretzels in quiet for a couple of easy moments.

Finally, Aidan inclined his head. "Okay, tell us already what's up so I can get to manscaping for my date."

Jake snorted.

Liam scowled. "I don't *manscape*. Just because I trimmed my eyebrows that *once*. You both should do the same, by the way. You both look feral." And they did. Aidan was in a worn-out blue T-shirt with more holes than fabric, and he had sawdust coating his hair. Jake was in a red flannel shirt that was ripped at both elbows.

"Come on, man. What's with the TV show?"

"They're for real, I think."

Aidan leaned forward. "They want to pay us to find, sell, and fix up houses. I don't see how that's different from what we already do. Except for the cameras. What's the point?"

"The point is money." Liam shot a finger gun at him. "A *lot* of money. More than we make all year.

The gal who's here to talk us into it said we should ask for double."

Jake shook his head. "There's a catch. There's always a catch."

"There is."

His brothers stared at him.

"We would have to date the buyers. While we're doing the work."

Jake's ungroomed eyebrows drew together. "That's a thing? That people would want to *watch?*"

"How should I know?" Liam didn't own a television—his last had broken seven years before and he'd never gotten around to replacing it. "Apparently their network owns a third of the reality shows on TV right now. They know what they're doing, supposedly."

Aidan brightened. "Sex on camera?"

"Like I said, totally feral."

"Because I would do that."

Liam took a deep breath. "No sex on camera."

"Damn."

"They pay for the dates. It sounds like we could get them to pay a lot for these dates. So if you've been wanting to go to New York for dinner, this would be your chance."

Jake stuck his legs out long and seemed to be inspecting his beat up boat shoes. "How does the girl pick which one of us to date? Because honestly, if she meets all of us, neither of you will have a chance."

Aidan snorted.

Liam said, "I have no idea. They seem to think this could be the new, hot thing. And if we manage to rake in the cash I think we can, we could finally open Ballard Youth. This would be our ticket."

Aidan and Jake both considered their beer bottles in silence. Liam understood their sudden quietness. Ballard Youth was a pipe dream, something they discussed over late-night shots and cigars on the back patio of the Golden Spike. It wasn't something they thought would ever really happen. When they won the lottery or their ship came in, they'd finally be able to open the after-school program for at-risk kids to honor the man who raised them. But buying the property, the house, getting the zoning and the state's blessing, hiring the staff that would be necessary—the sheer amount of cash that would be required to do all those things had left it nothing more than a pipe dream. Once, they'd gone far enough to open a joint checking account into which they all chipped in extra dollars as they had them. Liam was pretty sure there was almost a thousand dollars in the kitty. Enough for exactly nothing.

But too good to be true was usually just that. "It doesn't sound safe."

"I always wear a condom," said Aidan cheerfully.

Liam shook his head. "It's too easy. Do our job, and date, and get serious money? I don't trust it."

Aidan's face became serious. "It sounds outrageous. But dude, this is literally our dream." Liam nodded. "We'd have the money to keep the place funded for the first five years."

"Holy shit." Aidan rocked so far back he almost tipped over. "Where do we sign?"

Jake finally said, "You really think we could? Make it work?"

Liam said, "You're both actually okay with this? Including the dating?"

Aidan laughed. "This is TV. The women they choose will be pretty, if not drop-dead gorgeous. None of us are in relationships. Personally, I'm pretty sure I could get a girl to kiss me on camera *without* the promise of a rebuilt house to lure her into doing it."

Jake said, "Bill would do it."

Liam started. His brother was right. Bill, irreverent old Bill, would find it hilarious. "Oh, man. Are we really doing this?"

Aidan held up his beer. "To pretty ladies, and money that can do some good."

The brothers clinked bottles. Thom Grandy's boat chugged past on the way in for the night, raising a gentle wake. Overhead, the fog thinned enough that the full moon was a yellow glow.

But right now, just sitting in the clammy fog on the deck of his brother's boat was enough. Thinking about the fact that he'd have to have a meeting very soon with Felicia who was pretty enough to make his tongue feel tied each time he saw her filled him with a strange helium-like hope.

And Liam had always been very fond of hope, especially the kind that came out of nowhere.

NINE

When Felicia called the police department, she didn't expect the sheriff himself to show up. But Sheriff McMurtry said he was short-staffed and he'd take her report before going over to the city council meeting.

"This kind of thing doesn't happen all that often 'round here. Sorry that this is the way you were greeted."

"It's not a big deal. The rental agency wanted a report number." Felicia poked a black stuffed sheep with her forefinger and then, as she caught Pearl's sad gaze, regretted it. She gave the toy a one-fingered stroke and then felt ridiculous.

"Better to have this kind of thing on the record.

Pearl, you do make the best cup of coffee in town, I always say."

The innkeeper brightened, and Felicia respected the man's tact. The coffee tasted like old tea.

"Felicia, can you describe the kid again for me?"

The sheriff *looked* like a sheriff should, Felicia decided, dark and handsome and clean-cut. Maybe he'd gotten the job because of his looks. *No, this isn't Hollywood.* People didn't earn their jobs by the way they looked.

"He was big. Maybe my height."

"Which is..." Sheriff McMurtry held a silver pen above a yellow flip notebook.

"Six foot in heels, so I'd guess he was about that tall."

"Wow," he said admiringly. "Did you play basketball in high school?"

She shook her head. If she had a nickel for every time she'd been asked that. "But he was a lot heavier. Thicker." She put her hands at her neck. "Wide here. Oh, a red baseball cap."

The sheriff nodded. "Any writing on the cap?"

"White logo of some sort? Kind of round. It was too far away for me to see it clearly, though."

He looked up from his notepad. "Um. Did he... well, I don't want to lead you. But did he have anything else on his head?"

"Oh!" She'd almost left that out. "Glasses. Thick black-framed ones."

"Well, dang it."

"You know who it was?" She sat forward eagerly, and a stuffed sheep *baaaa*ed so loudly they both jumped.

"Maybe."

"Can we go to where he is?"

"Yeah. We can. But look, Ms. Turbinado, it's complicated."

"Oh, my god, is he your son?"

The sheriff's eyes widened and he touched his badge. "Me? Oh, no. But if it's the kid I think it was, he's had a rough go till the last year or so. He doesn't need more drama."

Didn't cops try to catch criminals, not save them? "I hear you. But he should have thought of that before he tagged my car."

"Okay. Look. We can do it the normal way, I write the report, you sign it. I take you to the department, and you look at a photo lineup and identify the kid you saw. It goes to the DA, and she decides whether or not to prosecute, and she will, even though it's just a misdemeanor, because not much happens here. Or we could do it my way. I'm going to ask you a big favor."

Felicia crossed her arms over her chest.

"Just think about it for a minute. Come with me

to the kid's house. We'll see if he's home, if it's even the kid I'm thinking of. We talk to him. See if we can find out what's up with him."

"This really is a small town, isn't it?"

"This isn't Los Angeles, Ms. Turbinado. The only gang in town is made up of seven square dancers who bully others into being their eighth." He stood. "Will you come with me? I bet we can clear this all up and help the kid be a better person at the same time. And if, after we talk to him, you still want to press charges, you can."

The boy *was* just a kid. And this would make a good dinner-party story later, the time she went with the local sheriff to catch a vandal. And it wasn't like she wanted the kid to do hard time breaking rocks in prison, just that she needed the police report for the rental agency. "Okay, fine. We can try it your way. In your car? I don't feel like driving a penis-mobile right now."

The sheriff smiled. "Lots of folks might call my ride that, too."

IN THE PATROL CAR, the sheriff whooped the siren for her once as he pulled onto the road. In front of them, the traffic (two cars and an old pickup truck) parted. "Does everyone ask you to do that?"

"Every single person who rides with me."

"I'm not unique then. But this place is, isn't it? What would you think of a reality show being set in your town?"

"*Oh,* no. No way." His words were fast.

"Take your time."

"Sorry. But in Darling Bay? That would be terrible."

"Why?"

"Because then people would know where we are."

"Isn't that what you want?" They drove past a yellow banner hanging from the front of city hall that read, *Congrats Darling Bay High School Grads! The World Awaits!* "I thought all small towns were just waiting to be discovered."

"Not us. We get too many damn tourists as it is."

"Isn't that good for your economy?"

"Sure. It's great for business. My girlfriend runs The Golden Spike Cafe."

"The place with the old caboose in front? I had a great latte there."

He nodded. "See? Everyone gets their coffee from her. The more tourists for her, the better. But for me, they just bring headaches. Big city people— no offense—don't seem to know what's important."

"Ah. Like vandalizing rental cars?"

"And that proves my point. This kid—if he is your suspect—is from the big city."

"Which one?"

"San Francisco. His parents were both junkies, dad dead, abandoned by mom at a methadone clinic. He's been in eight foster homes before winding up here in Darling Bay. If he manages to stay out of juvie, he has a real chance with this foster dad."

Felicia shook her head. "That's not on me, you know. I didn't make him tag my car."

"I know. And I don't want to pressure you about it. I'll let you make up your own mind. But I can tell the good apples from the bad, and he's a good one."

Kids weren't apples. But Felicia held her tongue, right up to the point where they pulled into the driveway she'd parked in that morning. *Ballard Brothers.* "Here? You're kidding me."

"You know Liam Ballard?"

"He's the only person I know in town besides you and Pearl. I spent the day with him. But he didn't mention a kid...oh." The sandwich drop off. "Crap."

"Come on, let's get this over with."

TEN

Opening the door to Felicia was a more-than-nice surprise. If Liam were honest with himself, he'd admit that he hadn't been able to get her off his mind since he'd dropped her off at her rental car.

Seeing Colin McMurtry behind her, though? That part wasn't ideal.

"Felicia. Colin. Is this the good kind of surprise or the bad kind? Come on in."

The sheriff didn't have to tell him, though—Liam could read it on his face.

Damn it.

"Timbo around, Liam?"

"Upstairs." Liam kept his voice even. If Timbo had done anything wrong, they'd have to go through him first. They could come this far into the kitchen, but they'd go no farther, not yet.

"Can we talk to you?"

"Seems like you already are." He crossed his arms over his chest and met Colin's gaze directly. How the hell was *Felicia* involved with something having to do with Timbo?

"You and Felicia Turbinado are already acquainted, is that right?"

He nodded at her, trying to ignore just how pretty she looked with all her hair bundled up on top of her head. "Just tell me what's going on."

"There's a chance Timbo vandalized her car."

He scowled at Colin. "How does she know it was him?" Jumping to defensive mode wasn't the best idea in the world, but he didn't see a way around it at the moment.

"She saw him do it. Or someone who sounds like him."

"Yeah, well, she doesn't know him."

Felicia took a step farther into the kitchen. "*She* is right here and would appreciate being spoken to instead of about. Is Timbo one of the kids we gave sandwiches to earlier?" Her brown eyes snapped dark heat at him.

This was bad. "Yeah."

"The one who likes his crusts off."

"Yeah."

"He wasn't wearing his glasses at the basketball court."

Liam's neck ached. Damn it. "He doesn't wear them there. He's broken two pairs already."

"But he wears them when he's riding his bike?" Felicia's face was steady, her lips firm. She didn't look angry, exactly, but she looked incredibly serious.

As well she should. "What did he do?"

"Egged my car—"

"That's not vandalism, not unless it broke something. It washes off, so it's just temporary damage. I'll have him—"

"*And* he decorated the car door with Sharpie," said Colin.

"Oh." *Crap.* "What did he draw?"

Felicia's dark eyes snapped sparks. "A penis."

Relief made him snort. He couldn't help it, and he regretted it immediately. "Sorry." He waved his hand in front of his face. "Totally unacceptable. I'll call him. Can you wait for me in the living room?" He gestured to the doorway, already headed up the stairs.

Of all people. Timbo had to choose her car?

Liam had *finally* thought Timbo was getting it— that when you lived in a town as small as Darling Bay, you hurt someone you knew when you broke the law. It was personal here, everything was about someone else.

Timbo had been doing so well.

Liam knocked once and entered Timbo's room.

"I saw the cop car." Timbo's voice was expressionless. He lay on his back in the middle of the double bed. "You want me to come down."

"I do."

"I didn't think. I wasn't thinking, I mean."

Liam tried to keep his anger where it belonged, right in the center of his chest, but it worked its way up to his larynx. "What the hell *were* you thinking?"

"It was a rental car. It said so right on the license plate holder."

"So that gives you immunity?"

"You *said*."

"Don't try to pin this on me." Liam kept his voice low. "I said the people in this town deserve your respect."

"But this wasn't—"

"The person who rented that car was *in* our town and therefore deserves our respect, too. *Why* did you do it?"

Timbo groaned and rolled over heavily. He buried his face in the pillow and said something Liam couldn't hear.

"Talk to me, not the pillow."

Timbo turned his head to the side. His cheek was wet. "I don't *know*. Okay? I'm just stupid. That's all. We already knew that."

Sometimes Liam forgot Timbo was only fourteen. "You're not stupid. You did a stupid thing."

"No difference."

"Big difference. But you hurt someone's property, and that matters. And now you get to make it right."

"No..."

"Come on down."

In the living room, Colin stood at the fireplace and Felicia sat on the big leather couch. Most people let themselves be swallowed up by the couch, which was the right way to sit in the comfortable beast, but Felicia was somehow managing to sit right on the very edge of it.

"Here he is." Liam stepped out of the way so they could see Timbo behind him.

"Timbo." Colin held out his hand for the boy to shake. Liam felt gratefulness—again—for the way Colin treated every single person in his path respectfully. "Good to see you."

Timbo nodded and stepped forward, not lifting his eyes. He shook the sheriff's hand. Then he hunched his shoulders, and he tugged the zipper on his hooded sweatshirt higher till it wouldn't go any further up his neck. At least he'd left the ball cap upstairs.

"This is Felicia," said the sheriff.

Timbo nodded.

"She's trying to decide whether or not to press charges for vandalism."

It hurt Liam's heart to watch the look on Timbo's face. The boy's eyes darted from Felicia to the sheriff and back again.

"I'm sorry," he mumbled. "I didn't mean to."

Felicia stood. She laced her fingers together in front of her. "Of course you did."

Liam wanted to step forward and protect him. How did other parents deal with this? He had a gut reaction—an intense *need* to shield the boy—and he'd only been in Timbo's life for two years.

But Timbo had screwed up.

"No—"

"It's not like you tripped and scribbled a penis on my car on the way down, is it?"

He shook his head.

"I didn't think so. So you meant to, even if you made up your mind at the very last minute." Felicia's face was fierce, her eyes dark. "I stole a car once."

Liam jumped, and Colin gave a bark of laughter that he turned into a cough.

Timbo stared. "You *did?*"

"I did. It was a pickup truck. I was so *angry* at my mom for forgetting me at school for like the twentieth time that year, and this old guy got out of his truck and left it running while he ran into the 7-11 across the street. I was furious, and I just wasn't thinking. At all. I got in, and I took it."

"Where did you go?"

"One block. I didn't know how to drive a stick shift, and when I finally got it into second, it stalled and I hit the side of a UPS truck."

"Whoa." Timbo looked horrified, and Liam was glad. "Did you get caught?"

"Are you kidding? The guy who owned the truck was like a million years old, but he grabbed my ear and held onto me until the cops got there."

"What happened to you?"

"I went to prison for six years."

Liam bit the inside of his cheek, and it looked like the sheriff was doing the same thing.

Timbo bought it, though. "Six *years?*"

"Okay, no. I'm lying to you. The guy let me off with a warning and a promise. I might do the same for you, *if* you think you're up for it."

Timbo looked at Liam. He was smart enough to be scared. Good. He'd better be. "What do you mean?"

Felicia shot a glance at Liam, but directed her words to Timbo. "If I stay in town, and I'm not sure

I will, I'll be working on a show. And I'll need help. You know what an intern is?"

Timbo shook his head slowly. He looked worried, as if he were about to take a pop quiz. "Something hospitals have?"

"Hospitals do have interns. It's kind of the same idea. You do work, for free, while you're learning. We usually have a couple on each of my jobs—in California, you can be one when you're fourteen, if it's your summer break and you have your guardian's permission."

Timbo shot a look at Liam. "What kind of work?"

"Working on my TV show."

Timbo jolted, like he'd tripped over something invisible. "I wanna do that."

"Again, I don't know if there *will* be a show. That's up to—" her gaze shot again to Liam "—that's up to some things I can't control right now. But if I do stay, you'll work for me. For free. To pay me back."

"Like, real TV?"

"Do I look familiar to you?"

Timbo tilted his head and squinted. He rubbed the cuff of his sleeve on his glasses. "Maybe one of those crime shows?"

"Nope. I'm never on screen. You'd be behind the scenes, like me. And it wouldn't be glamorous.

You'd be doing things like cleaning up after everyone else. Running things around, being a gofer."

"A gopher?"

"You would go-for the things we needed to have. Go-fer."

"I could do that. I could *totally* do that."

Wait a minute. Liam frowned. Was this going to feel like some kind of reward to Timbo? "I'm not sure—"

"Oh, don't you worry. If we do it, it's not going to be fun." Felicia lifted her chin. "And Timbo, if you stray out of line even once? I'm going to press charges instead of just filling out a property report without your name on it. You'll be arrested as fast as this nice officer can drive with his red light on."

"I won't screw up. I'm sorry I did what I did."

Liam rocked forward on his heels. "Go on up to your room now."

"Yes, sir." Timbo thundered up the stairs.

Felicia straightened her blouse. "Well. Okay."

"Thank you." The words were small, trivial, but Liam meant them. "I can't tell you—"

"Have you had a chance to talk to your brothers?"

He nodded.

"Maybe we can confer in the morning?"

Confer? What would it take for her to lose that

serious look on her face—the way she kept her mouth straight and her eyes all business? He'd seen a glimpse of the real Felicia in the Maupin house, when she'd kicked off her shoes and climbed up to the wooden platform. When she'd been telling him about her dream-game she'd played with her mother, she'd been as bright as a new penny. Now she was back to business.

"Yeah." He put a twang into his words on purpose as he attempted to get her to smile. "We don't confer 'round these parts. We do coffee. Sometimes we do lunch, and if it's a big ole meeting, we have beer with that lunch. You don't want to make things feel too fancy."

Felicia blew out a breath. "No need for fancy. Maybe coffee tomorrow?"

"You bet. Come by tomorrow, and we'll walk over to the Golden Spike Cafe." Ridiculously, Liam wanted her to stay longer. He wanted to feed her something hearty like spaghetti, something that would stick to her ribs and maybe make her look less pale. She had dark hollows under her eyes like she hadn't been sleeping well.

But Felicia Turbinado was already halfway to the door. She moved fast, as if she had someplace to be.

The sheriff said, "Now wait, I brought you, and I'll give you a lift back."

Felicia shook her head. "I'd like to walk. Clear my head a bit."

Liam couldn't just let her go just like that. "Hey. Can I feed you something? Dinner?" Liam heard Colin snort behind him. The man was sheriff for a reason—he didn't miss much. Liam would get ribbed for this later.

"I'm—I'm fine." She reached to shake his hand, and never had Liam wanted more to hug a stranger. But he didn't. He shook her hand professionally and steadily.

She met his eyes for a brief second. "Thanks for letting me talk to him."

"Thanks for not pressing charges." Liam felt gratefulness shoot through him again—he couldn't lose Timbo. Going to juvie would mean Timbo was lost, probably forever. "You're doing that kid a really big favor. I'll make sure he makes it right. Come by anytime in the morning. I'll be here."

Felicia nodded.

Then she was gone, leaving nothing behind but a light scent of jasmine.

Colin gave him a grin. "What do you think, pal?"

Without thinking, Liam said, "Damn, she smells good."

Colin laughed. "I haven't seen you stare at a girl like that in a long time."

"I wasn't staring."

"Your tongue was hanging out."

"Oh, shut up. Beer?"

Colin took off his badge and slipped it into his pocket. "As a matter of fact, I just got off duty. I'll tell you about the wreck that Terry Dunlap got in last week. Ended up in Teasley Pond. It was something, all right."

But as Liam got two beers out of the fridge, it wasn't the Dunlap crash he was thinking about.

Those big eyes of Felicia's—he figured he could sit on the porch and think about them for a few minutes.

And the rest of her?

Yeah, he could think about the rest of her for a while, too.

ELEVEN

Felicia felt as if she were sitting in the diner in Stars Hollow. Sadly, the handsome (and fictional, she reminded herself) Luke wasn't behind the counter—the person making the coffee and greeting customers was a woman, blonde and smiley and pretty. But the rest of the Golden Spike Cafe was as similar and old-fashioned as if the Gilmore Girls' set had been picked up and set down coast-side. Old mismatched wooden tables and chairs stood together companionably, and brightly colored surfboards hung on the walls. The menu was written in chalk on the wall, proudly proclaiming rosemary-chocolate muffins and a Joe's scramble with the works.

The coffee was perfect, strong and bitter with a

sweet high note. People chattered to each other and a busboy went red as he dropped and broke a coffee mug. The bell over the door jangled, and Felicia looked up just as she had the last fifteen times it had sounded.

Liam strode in, wearing a dark blue shirt worn open over a white T-shirt. His jeans fit him perfectly, stretching over his wide thighs. He looked like he should be wearing a cowboy hat, like half of the men who walked in the door were.

Felicia picked up her coffee mug to steady her hands, which were suddenly strangely jittery. Not like coffee would help with that problem, and she was probably about to spill it anyway. She set it down.

Liam waved at the hostess and clapped an older man on the shoulder. This was the kind of town where everyone smiled at *everyone* else. She'd noticed it on her walk to the cafe—people had not only grinned at her, which was alarming in and of itself, but they met her eyes, too. In LA, you only met someone's eyes if you wanted to yell at them or ask them out. Here, apparently, it was the norm. It had made Felicia feel anxious the first three times it happened but by the time she'd gotten to the cafe, she'd almost enjoyed it. She'd felt seen.

Turned out that was kind of nice.

Then Liam smiled at her, and Felicia felt something even better than nice.

"Good morning." He slid into the seat opposite her. "You got a booth. Someone must like you."

"Sorry?"

"Nikki McMurtry, the hostess over there, has a strict policy about these things. If she sees you kick a cat in an alley—"

"Who would do that?"

"Exactly, then you sit in that tiny middle table for the rest of your natural-born life. You only get a booth if you raise money for charity on your days off work."

"But she doesn't know me."

"She also likes a person with a pretty smile, and that you have."

Felicia felt it sneak across her face again. Felicia *had* beamed at the hostess when she'd walked in. The smell of coffee and cinnamon and bacon had made it impossible not to.

"Speak of the devil." Liam turned in his seat.

The blonde set an empty cup in front of Liam. "Good morning." She filled it with coffee without asking. "I hope you weren't saying anything bad."

"About you, Nikki? There's nothing bad to tell. Hey, this is Felicia Turbinado, a fancy network exec-you-tive." He strung out each syllable. "Felicia, this is Nikki McMurtry. She's also fancy, and one of the nicest people in town."

"Network? Like television or Netflix or something?"

"Yep."

"Are you doing a show here?"

Felicia chose her words carefully. "We might be. If the conditions prove right."

"The answer is yes, they are." Liam stretched his arms out over the back of the booth.

Nikki's eyes widened. "Oooh! In Darling Bay!"

Felicia's heart thumped, a strange reaction to a business decision. "We are, huh?"

"You bet."

Felicia opened her mouth and then closed it. She tried to swallow the grin but couldn't. She looked quickly at Nikki.

Nikki got the hint. "This is business, huh? Okay. I get you. Jackson will be by in a minute to take your order. And Liam, tell me everything later, all right?" With a wink she was gone.

Later? Felicia made a note to triple check later that Liam really was single, that if he was chosen by one of the women to be the love interest, that he was truly available. He'd said he was, and he didn't seem like a liar. But if Felicia had a dollar for every person she'd met in the last ten years who didn't seem like a liar but was, she wouldn't have to work ever again.

"So, you talked to your brothers last night?"

"I did."

"And you're all on board?"

"Pretty much. They'll want to go over terms and all of that when we get together to sign, and I'm sure they'll have questions, but it sounds good."

For a moment, Felicia felt guilty. Liam looked so positive, his eyes clear. He had no idea what reality TV might do to him, might do to the town. Best case scenario, the brothers would have fifteen minutes of fame which was uncomfortable but bearable. Worst case, they'd be launched into C-list-celebrity fame which had the potential to ruin people's whole lives.

"What is it?"

Felicia shook her head. "Nothing. I'm just pleased with your decision."

"No, there's something you're worried about."

She kept her voice light. "My job is to keep *you* from worrying."

"You're bad at your job, then." Liam's worn-denim eyes held concern. "I trust you to tell me what you're thinking."

He *trusted* her? Oh, lord. "I'm in show business. You should think twice about trusting anyone."

Liam pointed at the folder she'd put on the table. "That's paperwork for us to go over?"

"Yes."

"I trust that you have the network's best interests at heart."

"I—yes." That's what he should be worried about.

"But I also trust that you're a good person, and that you're not going to rip us off."

Felicia bit her bottom lip for a second. "We don't rip people off. We compensate them fairly. And in your case, I wrote the prelim contract at double the rate you talked about with Natasha, like I mentioned."

"Great."

"It's just that—" She pressed her back against the leather of the booth.

"Tell me."

Fine. She would. There was something so innocent about this man, and Felicia felt protective, suddenly. "Sudden fame can make people do stupid things."

"You're saying we're going to be dancing with the stars next?"

"Heck, that's good money if you can get it. I'm saying I've seen people take it hard—going from ultra-famous back to being nobody is difficult."

Liam's face lit up. "Shoot. I'm used to being nobody."

"It's just—" She reached a hand forward unthinkingly and to her vast surprise, Liam caught it. She wanted to pull it back, but she didn't. His hand was wide, his grip firm and warm.

"Go on."

"I've seen people hit the rocks. Latent alcoholism goes full-blown. People who used to like to spend quick weekends in Vegas with their spouses go there alone and blow not only their TV earnings but the mortgage payment, too. It can be ugly, and it can happen fast."

"You don't have to worry about me. The most I'm likely to do is throw away a huge wad at the Bingo hall, but that's only if Sweetie Swensen riles me up and that's something she likes to do anyway, just for fun." Liam's thumb stroked the back of Felicia's hand.

Goosebumps rose on her arms, and she hoped he didn't notice. She should pull her hand back—and at the same time, she wanted to sit like this with him for the next hour. Or ten. "Okay. But what about your brothers? What's the money going to do to them?"

"Aidan will use it to buy some dumb tool that hoists something else. Jake might go on a bender, though."

"Yes. Exactly. That's the kind of thing I'm worried about."

"But Jake's kind of bender means he heads out on his sailboat for Fiji and comes back a few months later, looking browner and skinnier and happier."

Really? Grounded, healthy men? They really existed?

What if the show *was* enough to break them?

Felicia darted a look around the cafe, and suddenly felt the weight of fifty stares on them. This local guy was holding her *hand*. Did the people watching them think they were on a date?

She pulled her hand back, and shoved the folder forward. "This is the preliminary contract. You want to have your lawyers to look it over, of course, though I can assure you our legal team is the best in the business. We want to make you happy, that's what this is all about." Felicia felt stupid just saying it. This wasn't about making the Ballard Brothers happy. It was about making the network money by luring in advertisers, that was all it was ever about. Commercials: buying them, getting them, keeping them. Just as Felicia liked to think of toast as a butter-delivery provider, television programs were a vehicle for commercial consumption.

Liam nodded slowly. "I'll have Doug King look at it."

"He's your legal counsel?"

"He's my scuba buddy, but he has a law degree, I know that for sure. At least I'm pretty sure that's what he said."

"Are you serious?"

"He's smart. Don't worry. And I'm *pretty* sure he has actual clients."

Only slightly relieved, Felicia took a sip of her coffee. "Look it over. I can meet you and your brothers later today, if that works, or tomorrow is fine, as well."

"We're in a hurry?"

"The network is always in a hurry."

"That's fine. I can glance it over for starters right now, if you want." Liam open the folder and lowered his head to it.

She could see the comb lines at the top of his head where his hair was still wet. Over the scent of bacon and eggs, she could smell something better, more manly. Aftershave? Something piney and minty. Delicious.

He flipped more pages. He sipped his coffee absentmindedly. She wondered if he always took it black, or if there were mornings he liked cream and sugar, or a latte, maybe. Was he the kind of guy who liked to lie in bed on a Sunday morning with the paper, his hand resting on the hip of the woman next to him?

Liam turned the last page. "I'm meeting with

my brothers this afternoon to sign. Anything you forgot to tell me?"

So had he just skimmed the physical contact clause? Felicia felt her cheeks go red. She held up her coffee mug, hiding behind it. "Maybe."

"Who's the woman going to be?"

Relief was sweet. Not about the clause, then. "We have a list of women who've expressed interest in buying in the area."

"And she'll pick the house."

"Yes." *Any house but the treehouse.* Felicia wouldn't be able to bear watching it go to someone else. She'd talk Natasha out of even listing it as a possibility. Hopefully.

"And she'll pick the guy."

"Yes."

"What if she picks Aidan and he doesn't like her?"

"Then it'll be awkward as hell and it'll make for great television."

Liam nodded. "Surprisingly honest."

"I like truth."

"You work in television."

It didn't feel like the right time to get into her television-displays-true-reality speech. "Yeah, well. Are all three of you really, truly single?"

He held up his hand, palm out. "Scout's honor."

"Okay." She was perhaps gladder than she should have been.

"Are you?"

"Me?" Her voice came out in a squeak.

"You."

"Um. Yes. Why?"

Liam settled back into the booth. "I was just wondering. Maybe *you* should buy the treehouse."

Felicia smiled at the thought of living here. Near this man with the eyes she felt she could drown in. "I wish."

"Sometimes wishing makes a thing true."

Well, hell. She'd wish a little harder, then.

TWELVE

His brothers stopped by the office that afternoon to sign the papers.

"You already read every page, right?" Aidan jabbed his thumb on the end of his pen so hard the pen flexed. "Because Quincey got locked up in Kalamas on an old traffic warrant, and until he's out, I'm a pair of hands short. I only have a minute to do this."

"What, you think I haven't read it?" Liam was offended. All he did was look at papers. All day long. He read every line of everything that crossed his desk.

Jake shook his head. "Nah, of course you did. We just wanted to make sure you didn't miss a page or something, all distracted by whats-her-name."

"Felicia."

"Yeah, her."

Liam would protest, but his brothers would see through it. Felicia *was* distracting as hell.

Aidan scowled. "What if the women they choose for us are just straight-up witches? Or nightmare clients? We can't dump them?"

"They'll be fine, I'm sure." Liam wasn't sure. But shit, how *would* they release a bad client? Could they? "Give me that."

Jake scrawled his signature before handing him the packet of papers. "I don't care who these women are. They'll come in, we'll fix up a house for them, go on a couple of all-expenses paid dates, and then we cash the checks. As long as the money is green, I don't give a crap."

"Hang on." Liam flipped through the pages he'd skimmed in the restaurant right after Felicia left. "Let me just—oh, damn."

"What?"

His eye ran down a column of numbers. "I didn't read this page."

Jake dropped the pen onto the desk like it had burned him. "What did I just sign?"

"Don't worry—we'll just rip it up if we disagree with it. Hang on." He read faster and flipped the page. "This is impossible. No."

"What?" Aidan craned his head.

"It's a list of potential bonuses."

"I like bonuses."

"Attached to...What the *hell?* Attached to sexual acts?"

Aidan hooted. "Damn, I hope so! A bonus for a job well done!"

But it wasn't funny to Liam. How had he missed this whole page?

First kiss: five thousand dollars.

Every kiss thereafter: five hundred dollars.

Sex, off-camera, with bedroom pre- and post-filming: ten thousand dollars. Must be consensual and not the intended purpose of making money (see California Penal Code 647(b)).

"Ten *grand?*" Aidan stopped reading over Liam's shoulder and took a step back. "I thought you meant like fifty bucks. Bonus for good work."

Liam stared. "You have a price that's okay with you, and it's low? Not high?"

"Hell, yes, I do. Fifty bucks is a nice bottle of wine. That's a normal bonus."

"For *you.*" Liam looked at Jake. "Do you get gratuities for sex?"

Jake shrugged. "It's not like I've been putting out a tip jar."

"Ten grand is sex work." Aidan tugged on his belt loops. "I'm a contractor. Not a gigolo."

"Go." Liam shuffled the contract's papers. He

was an idiot, distracted by a pretty girl. He would read every page over, line by line. "Get to the site. I'll fix this."

LIAM DIDN'T EVEN HAVE to go inside the Cat's Meow to find Felicia Turbinado. She was sitting on a small balcony that overhung the front garden. She had glasses on, paperwork in her hand, and a computer in her lap.

She looked serious. Smart.

She looked cute as hell.

And he wasn't in the mood for cute.

"Is that our contract you're looking at?" His voice wasn't exactly a yell, but it wasn't quiet, either.

She jumped and leaned over the railing. "Hey, there! Yeah, it is. Hang on, I'll come let you in."

A moment later, she opened the front door. "You want to talk in the day room? It's covered with stuffed animals and smells like a Strawberry Short-cake doll, but I think there's coffee already made." She was wearing black leggings and a long black top that was cut low enough to distract a man. Her feet were bare—this was the second time he'd gotten a look at her dark red nail polish. Her hair was damp, as if she'd exercised and then showered.

"I've had coffee." He saw Pearl Hawthorne pop her head out of the kitchen briefly. The woman had ears too big for her head and a mouth to match. "We should talk in private."

"Is there a problem?"

"You could say that."

Felicia nodded, and her expression went from friendly to blankly professional. As she led him up the stairs and into her room, she could have been ushering him into a dentist's office. "Right in here. Please don't mind the stuffed animals. How about on the deck? It's the only place I don't feel like I'm going to suffocate."

"Sure." He followed her outside, taking the plastic chair. It was still wet from dew—he felt it soak into the back of his jeans. He winced.

"This is about the contract?"

"How did you not point out page seventy-one to me?"

"Ah. The physical-contact clause."

Liam gripped the plastic arm of the chair and moved it with a loud scraping noise. He needed to face her for this. "The sex-for-money clause, you mean?"

She turned her chair so that they were almost knee to knee. "That's definitely a misread. I'm sorry, we should have gone over that in person."

"You think? Ten thousand for sex, off camera? What the hell do you pay for sex *on* screen?"

Felicia shook her head. "That's not allowed. We don't have the licensing for that."

He could practically hear the *unfortunately* she left off the end of the sentence. "Is this in every contract?"

She smiled. Yeah, she must be good at her job. That smile could get an octogenarian to sign a thirty-year mortgage. "Of course."

"So this is a *thing?*"

"We have other shows that are comparable in scope and mission, and yes, this is a boilerplate contract. Of course, we can negotiate."

"See, here's the thing." Liam felt heat creep along his spine. "Me and my brothers aren't prostitutes."

A light laugh. "The money is just a bonus. Our lawyers have strictly vetted the language, and it's not against any state penal code. We're very careful. And you could of course agree beforehand with the buyer what you'd both allow or disallow."

Did she not get it? "Come on. What if *you* were the buyer?"

"What?" Her eyebrows flew upward in what looked like horror.

"Just think about it. You want the treehouse,

you buy it. We fix it up. You pick one of us to *have sex with for money*. How would *you* feel?"

"I don't...I can't buy a house."

Liam ground his teeth together. "No, this isn't about the house. It's about—"

"But what if I *did* buy it?"

He stared. "What?"

Felicia stood as she were going inside, and then sat again. Her eyes flared wide. "I want the treehouse."

Liam felt a hollow thump inside his chest. "Can you...can you *do* that?"

She shook her head. "I don't think so. It *has* to be against the rules, and I've looked. But I can't find anything about it in the contract. Or in any of our other contracts. It's never come up." Her hands flew to her cheeks. "I'm not thinking about this. No. I'm being crazy."

Liam realized that if Felicia bought the treehouse, then she'd be the woman with the bought-and-paid kisses on the line.

Huh. Funny. He was suddenly much more amenable to the contact clause.

Her forehead uncreased, and she reached to grab her laptop from the small glass table. "No, I'm not going to do that. Okay, we're talking about the bonus schedule. Sure. We had a contestant on our *Lost and Naked* show who wouldn't accept that we had a bonus built in for nighttime cuddling, and I'm trying to remember what we replaced it with—"

"*Felicia.*" Was it his imagination or did she feel the electricity that crackled between them, too? Like a storm moving in off the ocean—he could almost smell the sharpness of it.

She jerked up her head and met his gaze. "Yes."

"Let's just say you did it. Bought the house. Had us fix it up."

"But I have a condo. In LA."

"So call it a vacation home." She probably had the money.

"But I have a *job*, also in LA."

"If you bought the treehouse, how would you feel about the contact clause?"

"Um." She tilted her head and appeared to be stalling. "I guess it would depend on the brother."

Liam didn't hesitate. "Me. Say it's me."

"Oh." The word was breathy.

"So me kissing you. For the first time. Five thousand dollars?"

She grabbed the contract, and flipped the pages. "Okay. Sure, but no one says you have to kiss anyone. It's just a potentiality."

Liam leaned forward over the paperwork.

Her head came up quickly.

And in just the right place.

Without thinking too much about it, without

wondering if he should stop himself, Liam put his hand behind her neck and kissed her.

For a split second, she tensed in surprised. She gasped against his mouth, her neck muscles rigid. He stilled so he wouldn't frighten her.

Then she leaned into him. She tasted like peppermint and honey. Her lips were as charged as the air around them. As her mouth moved against his, as her fingers tangled in his hair, he realized he was in control of nothing at all.

She gave a quiet groan in the back of her throat. He was suddenly so hard it hurt. And the kiss was becoming something else, something he couldn't predict.

He pulled back.

Felicia blinked and touched her lips. "What the *hell* was that?"

"Just getting five thousand dollars out of the way, in case you end up being the client. That's the first kiss, right?" Oh, he liked the sound of that. It implied there would be a second kiss and a third and fourth and a hundredth and a thousandth.

Every single one of those he wanted.

Felicia stared up at him blinking, as if she'd never seen him before. "What?"

Some women were made for fun, for speed, for a nice friendly sexual hit-and-run. That kind of woman didn't scare Liam.

This kind did. This woman's eyes said to believe her. Then she'd leave and go back to where she'd come from.

He could fall in love with a girl like this.

So each and every one of those kisses that he wanted would be a bad idea.

He touched the balcony railing to steady himself. "That was the wrong thing to do."

"I have to agree with you on that one." But her words were breathy, and her chest rose and fell in the same rhythm as his.

Bad idea or not, Liam liked kissing this woman.

Felicia rubbed her forehead, as if it suddenly hurt. "I can't buy the house. I'm not—anyway. Okay, I'll be in LA for the next three weeks while we work on casting the client—I'll talk to Natasha about getting that clause removed, but honestly, I doubt she'll go for it..." She touched her bottom lip, and then looked up at him. Her eyes were dark pools of heat. Something inside his chest tugged tightly, as if there were a string between his body and hers.

She was leaving for three weeks, and of course she was. "Yeah." He needed to run, to get out. It was cowardly but who cared?

Felicia stood and pushed back her chair, so he'd have enough room to get around her. But the thought of being so close to her, of going through that terrible chintz-filled bedroom again, of making his way down the stairs that smelled of old rose petals and strawberry jam made Liam shudder.

So he just said, "I'll see you."

Then he sat on the balcony railing, swung his legs over, and in a move he and his brothers had perfected over the years, twisted himself so that he was hanging from the edge of the railing with his hands. He stretched his body as far as he could to the ground, and at the last minute, he let go. He absorbed the shock with his knees, and knew that he'd feel it in his right ankle tomorrow.

Felicia spoke from above. "Really?"

It didn't matter what she thought. She'd be gone for three weeks, and surely in that time, he'd figure out a way to be around this woman without losing his mind.

Right now it mattered only that he got away from her.

She made him feel something he'd wished to never feel again.

Hope.

THIRTEEN

"Did you get the email I sent you last night?" Natasha, as usual, was doing three things at once—walking at her treadmill desk while editing show notes and haranguing Felicia, who was sitting on the office couch, going through applications. It seemed like a lot of single women wanted to own property close to a beach. And close to three handsome brothers. Felicia shuffled through the men's headshots, pairing them idly with applicants. Did rugged Aidan look better with a blonde or a brunette? Who wouldn't want to kiss a handsome Ballard brother?

Felicia had kissed one, after all.

And Liam had *leaped off a balcony* to get away from her.

That was a low point for kissing, even for Felicia, who'd had some spectacularly bad kisses in her life. The sad thing was that it had been a phenomenal kiss, really one of the best, even as ill-advised as it was. It had been intensely hot. Knee-knocking. Scorching. Until he'd leaped.

Natasha tossed a sharp look over her shoulder. "Hello?"

"Yes, I got the email." Felicia had been ignoring it, that was all.

"I want the treehouse."

"We can want whatever property we want, but we can't make our client buy something she doesn't want, can we?"

"Why not? What does legal say? Can we sell it for her after we wrap if it's not the one she wants?"

"No." That wouldn't be fair to whoever was chosen.

Natasha's stride grew quicker and she pushed her straight black hair over her shoulders. "Treehouse. It's perfect, you can't tell me it's not. It's so run down that a whole remodel will show incredibly well on camera. Plus you have the whole novelty thing going for it. People will eat that shit up. We'll find a pretty treehugger who's looking to start a new life in a small town. Oh! What if she hits it off, like for real, with one of the brothers? Do you think we can add a wedding bonus?"

"It's too small. Tiny rooms." Felicia fumbled in her purse for the emergency granola bar she usually kept in it. "And the newer house has a view of the water. The treehouse doesn't."

"Nothing in that town could be too far from the water, right?"

Natasha was right. That was the galling thing. They could legitimately include shots of the marina, no matter which property they went with. "The treehouse looked like it was about to fall down."

"Even better. With luck, they'll find something majorly structurally wrong, and have to scramble to fix it. It's *perfect*."

"You can't." Felicia couldn't help the words.

"Sorry?"

Natasha wasn't sorry, Felicia knew. That was the very edge of Natasha's scary voice. Felicia should tread carefully, or she'd have to woo not only the brothers to do the show, but her boss to get back into her good graces. "I mean, it's just not a good idea. You didn't see the place."

"There's something you're not telling me."

Felicia grimaced. Then she took a breath. "No, it's just not right for us. Trust me."

"I have no intention of trusting you. Not now. Not with whatever this is you're not telling me. Spill."

"Nat—"

Her boss shot her another glance over her shoulder. "What happened? They're all alcoholics? I mean, I met them in a bar, and that older brother was drunk as hell, but he'd just been jilted."

"They're not alcoholics. Well, at least not that I could tell."

"What is it? They're part of a polygamous cult? Because that could work too. I'm ready to shape this show into a moneymaker, and I know you've got my back. Right?"

Maybe just chewing on something would help. Felicia stuck a piece of gum in her mouth. "Sure."

"Then what?" Natasha jabbed at the face of her phone.

"I want it."

"What?"

"The house."

"For yourself?" Natasha hit the stop button and let the treadmill carry her to its edge. "You can't do that."

Felicia couldn't agree more. "Obviously."

Natasha's voice was even sharper than her gaze as she stepped off the machine. "You have a life in LA."

"I do."

"And a job. The best job in the world, which is working for *me*."

"True." Most days Felicia loved working for Natasha. She was fast and regimented and oftentimes difficult, but she got the job done, and she didn't apologize for doing things her way. She was a champion and a fighter, and Felicia had thought she'd wanted to be just like her.

Until this afternoon.

Natasha took a quick sip of water. "You're suffering holidayitis. You know, when you go to Hawaii and you love it so much you think you want to buy a house there, and then you find out that gas is like twenty dollars a gallon and lizards live on inside walls."

"Geckos."

"Whatever. They're horrible. What you really want is to make a shit-ton of money on this show, because you're a sensible person and my very favorite employee."

Felicia sat on the very edge of the sofa. She made her back ramrod straight. "I want the house."

Natasha took an audible breath. "Okay. Because you're my friend, explain this to me."

Were they friends? Felicia had never been quite sure. "It's going to sound stupid, and I'm not even going to try to sugar-coat it. I had a dream about it when I was little."

"About this house."

"It can't be, I know that, but it was close enough to my dream to be really spooky."

"Hmmm." It was a dismissive sound. "It's a huge coincidence."

"It is. I know that. If I imagined another house right now, I know it would actually exist some-where. There're just not that many ways to put to-gether a house." That was what she'd been telling herself since they left the property. It was just com-monsense. If you imagine something, somewhere it existed just because it was *possible*. That's how doppelgängers worked—there were only so many ways to put together a human face.

And even as Felicia told herself that, she couldn't help think it was her house. Where she'd finally be home, and live a real life, one that had nothing to do with hiding behind television. "So that's why I can't support using this house for the show. I'm going to buy it."

"What about your job?"

Was that a threat in Natasha's voice? Felicia gripped her pen tighter. "Call it my vacation house."

"Can you afford it?"

"Yes."

"What if you lose your job?" It *was* a threat.

Felicia's heart fluttered in her chest. "I have money put away. It's the perfect house for me, even if I don't live in it now. I can rent it out or put it on Airbnb."

Natasha shook her head, as if disappointed in her. "Perfect doesn't exist. That's your problem. You're always hoping that Prince Charming will swoop in on his white horse."

The image of Liam rose in Felicia's mind. He'd look good on horseback.

And wow, was that ridiculous.

"It's just a house, Natasha, not a prince. I saw it first. I'm going to buy it. You need to choose another house for the show's selection. This one is mine." Even as she said it, it felt right. It was a fantasy, yes, just like the shows she loved and helped create. But this was the first time she'd felt like she could make the fantasy come true.

"Goddammit, Felicia. What's it going to take for me to convince you to put this house on camera? Do *you* have to be the target buyer for the episode?"

Felicia laughed. "Don't joke. I thought about it."

Natasha was silent, and the space above her upper lip went white. It only went like that when she was thinking about something that would mean a lot more work for Felicia.

Oh, no. "I was just joking—"

"That's exactly it. Did you film when you were there?"

"Of course not." She'd been scouting. Not filming.

"That's fine, we can have you run through it again. You think you could act like you'd never seen it before?"

"No! I'm not an actress." And she wasn't interested in becoming one.

"Yes. This is wonderful. Which guy do you want to date while they're redoing the house?"

"What? None of them." *Liam.*

She could see Natasha shifting into high gear. "We'll pay you, of course."

"Natasha—" She would not get steamrolled by her boss.

"A lot." Natasha named a figure that would cover the entire down payment.

"You can't—" But Felicia had lost her breath. If that's where Natasha *started* negotiations?

"Just a bonus."

"It's not morally right. To have a producer be the talent?"

"That's true. You're fired."

The tips of Felicia's fingers went numb as a chill ran through her. "*What?*"

"I'll rehire you when the episode is in the can. I *love* it. We can advertise it that way, too. The house that a producer was willing to be fired to have. I'll have to re-fire you on screen, of course."

"*I am not an actress.*"

"Two lessons. That's all it takes. I'll get you Angelina's guy. She couldn't act her way out of a paper bag till he got his hands on her. Anyway. Which guy?"

"I've only met Liam."

"Hot, hot, hot. Not as dirty-hot as the other two, but if you want a guy in a suit, he's the one you should go for."

"I'm not going to date a guy on camera."

"You don't have to sleep with him on camera, for crying out loud. Off camera, though, of course, would be nice for us. What's the big deal?"

The big deal? Felicia lost the air in her lungs as she imagined Liam naked. Those shoulders—she'd been able to see their definition right through his shirt, and she'd wondered if he was as well-defined all the way down. His hands—so big and wide—on her body, moving, stroking... No, what was she thinking? "That's basically prostitution, you know. Paying a woman to hook up with a guy just so she can have a little more cash to put toward a house?"

"Don't forget, you loved this idea." Natasha pointed a thin finger at her. "You're our target market, that's one of your best qualities. You think this stuff is real."

"It can be."

"My darling girl."

They made fantasy shows, yes. Felicia could admit that. But the love that happened as a result could be real and lasting and true. She just *knew* it.

So maybe a fantasy house could be obtained in a fantasy way.

It would still be her house. She would just be getting it in a different way, a way she hadn't planned on. She'd be using the show to acquire it.

Or would she be using Liam Ballard? Was that right? Fair?

"What's the real problem here?"

"He is. Liam Ballard. There's no way he'll swallow the contact clause." It was a lie—she'd already told him they could negotiate and she knew they could. The *real* problem was that Felicia fell in love with men on reality shows as often as she could. It was her favorite thing to do, bar none. But this time the man was real, flesh and blood. Felicia wouldn't be sitting on her couch, watching, popcorn bowl at her left, remote at her right. She wouldn't be at work, setting up the shot. She would be *in* the shot. *She* would be the one making innocuous comments that the producers would twist into something more, something embarrassing, or worse, something vacuous.

And Felicia herself, the real girl, would tumble head over heels for Liam. She knew herself too well.

She just wasn't cut out for real life. She never had been.

"Look." Natasha's voice was softer now, and she dropped into a cross-legged position in front of Felicia. "I get it. It's scary, thinking about being on the wrong side of the camera. We're hidden when we're on this side, yeah? The end justifies the means, though, doesn't it? You love that house. And I'm your champion. I want you to get that house, the vacation home of your dreams. I can't wait for you to show me around. I bet you'll fit into that little old small-town like you were born to be there. You'll wear fancy aprons, and be the hit of the bake sale."

Felicia blinked hard. Unsure if it was a compliment or an insult, she let herself wonder: what would that be like? To be a real part of the town, to live where people knew her name, said hello to her on the street?

"You still haven't given me a good reason why you won't do it."

Because I would fall in love with him. Because he's real. Because he kisses like an angel on rumspringa. "I just don't want to." God, how juvenile. It wasn't an answer.

The color came back to Natasha's face, something that happened after she'd made up her mind about something. She leaned forward in a graceful stretch, digging her fingers into the deep white carpet. "I want that house for the show. It's not up for debate. You're doing this."

Felicia's breath was tight. "Or—"

"Or I fire you right now for real and get Melody up there on the next flight."

"You can't—"

"I can. I'm within my legal rights. I want this to be epically global. With you on the show, it will be."

"It'll be terrible."

"Darling. It's not like you have to *marry* one of them."

Oh, god.

Felicia was going to be on a reality show.

FOURTEEN

Timbo was usually happy to help Liam in the kitchen, but tonight he was even brighter, like he was made of sparks—all flickering joy. He ran from one side of Liam to the other, grabbing things that Liam might need to make the lasagna, happy to put them back when he didn't.

"You know dinner won't be ready for a while, right?"

"I had a Snickers. What about the show?"

"We can talk about it later. Why don't you tell me how your day was? Did you guys beat the Triple Diamonds?"

Timbo's face fell, and Liam regretted bringing it up. "They creamed us."

"Sorry about that, champ."

"Whatever." Then he brightened. "So, what about that show? Can I really work on it? Like she said?"

"We'll see."

If Liam had thought Timbo's face had fallen a moment before, this time it went all the way to the floor. "We'll *see*?"

"I might have pissed off the producer." What he'd done was kiss the producer and then run away.

"I thought this was the only way you could afford to open Ballard Youth."

Liam set down the jar of tomato sauce, not caring that some of it glopped to the countertop. "You were eavesdropping?"

"No." Timbo crossed his arms.

"Remember we talked about that?"

"No."

"Really? Because I think you do, and I don't think you want to have that conversation with me again, do you?"

"No." His jaw shot sideways like it did when he was frustrated.

"Okay, then. No more of that."

"God." Timbo pushed himself away from the counter and stumbled backward until he landed in a chair at the table. "Did you see that? I *totally* almost fell."

"But you lived."

A pause. "Can you un-piss her off?"

"I honestly don't know where we stand with her." Contracts were signed. Paperwork was bouncing back and forth. Nothing had come up about Timbo interning. It was possible Liam had just blown it all. "We can't control the universe. Remember, we talked about that?"

Timbo lowered his head to the tabletop melodramatically. "Man, you gotta come up with some new material, all you do is go over what we already said."

"It'll be fine. Just don't set your heart on it, okay?" Liam pulled three cloves of garlic off the bulb, and smashed them with the side of his knife.

"Oh, man, are you going to pull out of the show? You'll be *famous*."

"I never wanted that."

"But the *money*. Where else are you going to get that?"

"Paper route?"

"You know, grades are more important than you think." Timbo's eyes were wide, his expression guileless. "Maybe you could go back to school. Get a degree in something important."

"You planning on stopping the jackass routine anytime soon?"

"Nah. This is fun."

Liam twisted his lips to keep the smile from

taking over his face. This kid. Sometimes Liam wondered how it was that people had overlooked Timbo for so long. Why did he get to be the lucky one that took care of this guy? How had he been ignored, unseen?

Instead of saying it, though, he just kept chopping garlic.

Timbo thumped the floor with his shoe. "That girl is pretty."

"Who?"

"You're bad at playing dumb."

That was probably the biggest problem with Timbo—you couldn't get anything past the kid. He'd probably noticed exactly how Liam had reacted to Felicia. "Yeah, I guess she is."

"When are you gonna see her again?" Timbo picked up a paper napkin and started shredding it into tiny pieces.

"She'll be back in three weeks to talk to us some more. We'll see then—"

"Do you believe in love at first sight?"

Liam stopped chopping and turned to look at him. "What are you talking about? Where did you even get that idea?"

"Some stupid movie I saw at Roger's house. The guy walks into a mall and sees a blonde and the rest of the movie is about him chasing her around. I kind of thought he was acting like a stalker, but eventually the girl liked it. That seems kind of dumb, you know?"

"Yeah." Liam went back to chopping and almost took off the end of his middle finger. That was a useful one. He didn't want to lose it. He slowed his motions.

"You didn't answer my question, though. Do you? Believe in it?"

"Kiddo, I have no idea."

Timbo slumped into the chair as if gravity had suddenly become too much to bear. "I knew you would blow it. She'll never let me intern."

"Thanks for the vote of confidence."

"This could be the most important thing to ever happen to you."

For a second, Liam thought Timbo meant his meeting Felicia. The most important thing to ever happen to Liam. The knife came dangerously close to the tip of his finger again.

Timbo went on, "You might end up being famous, and then *I* would be famous, and then I'd probably get a scholarship playing basketball to Notre Dame or something awesome like that. Our whole lives could be different if you don't blow this."

"How does my selling a house to a woman on national television make you into a better basketball player?"

Timbo shrugged. "So tell me *why* you're all freaked out and stuff."

Maybe it was okay to be honest with him. Liam remembered a time long ago, when Bill had been honest with him about why Liam and his brothers had to walk to school. *It's because I lost my license. I did something stupid, drove home from work after having a couple of beers with the boys.*

You drove drunk?

I did. Do you know why that was stupid?

Because it's illegal?

That doesn't necessarily make it stupid. But I was behind the wheel of that dumb old truck and I shouldn't have been. If a little kid had run out in front of my car, I might've killed him. It was probably one of the stupidest things I've ever done, and now I'm not going to have a license for a while. I'll keep the truck, but just for you all to learn on. That means you all have to walk for a while. For that, I'm sorry.

Bill had looked heartbroken, and now that Liam was a grown man with a foster kid that he loved of his own, he could hardly imagine being that honest about a mistake that big. He kept Bill's old rusty truck in front of the house as a reminder of the man —of what honesty and love looked like. Maybe it wasn't pretty and maybe it was kind of beaten up, but like Bill, it was reliable and sturdy. He wished he could tell Bill how much that confession had meant to him. Liam had never driven drunk, not once, not even when he was twenty-one and stupid as a stick.

So, maybe in honor of Bill, he'd be honest with Timbo. "I guess it has a lot to do with Brandy."

"Brandy? But she's not even around."

"Maybe I'm scared of being hurt again." This was stupid. A fourteen-year-old boy wouldn't understand this. He couldn't be expected to.

"Yeah, well, she was a bitch."

"*Excuse* me?"

Timbo sat up straighter in his chair. "You can't be mad at me. I'm just quoting what Uncle Aidan said."

Liam put the flats of his palms against the countertop. "Uncle Aidan shouldn't have said that about her. We do *not* talk about women like that. You get me?"

Timbo had the grace to look chastened, and his gaze dropped to his lap. "Sorry. But I don't think she should have said yes to your proposal if she was just going to run away the night before. The girls at school call her the Runaway Bride. Someone said it was an old movie, but it's not one I want to see."

It wasn't a movie Liam wanted to see, either. He'd lived it. He didn't feel like watching a rerun. And that, right there, was why he didn't want to be around a woman who made him feel the way Felicia did. In two whole years of being with Brandy, kissing her had never felt as electric as that one damn kiss he'd planted on Felicia. Brandy had been a safe choice. A good choice. Another realtor, she understood the business. He'd thought she'd understood him, too. But when she'd called him the night before their small wedding was supposed to occur, she'd told him that he'd never *seen* her. "You never let me in. You never trusted me to stay." He hadn't pointed out the obvious, that she wasn't. "You and your brothers, they're all that matter to you. When they need you, you drop everything and go running." The unfair part was that she'd never asked him to drop a damn thing. She'd just been there. Until she wasn't.

Liam went back to chopping the garlic even though it was finer than a mince now, and in a minute it would be a paste. "Remember when Sarah babysat overnight? And I came home with that hangover—which are even worse than they look, by the way, they make you want to die—that was the night I was celebrating a year of singleness. I've gotten over Brandy, you know."

"How?"

Hanging with his brothers. Some tears. Some anger, and some resignation. "Sometimes it just takes time."

Timbo scratched his head. "How long did it take you to get over your mom leaving?"

"I don't know, kiddo. Do you ever get over something like that?" The knife slipped for the third time. This time it nicked his first finger. "Dammit." Liam sat at the table and twisted a paper towel around the end of his finger.

"I'll get the Band-Aids!" Timbo thundered from the room. He was probably excited to get the bandages for a wound that wasn't his own.

His mother. Some wounds were just too deep. Maybe that's what made Liam love Timbo so hard —he understood that pain of having a mom take off, a mom who chose a life that didn't include the person she was supposed to love above all others.

Timbo ran back in the room. "We only got the Superman kind, but here's a big one."

"You're the best."

Timbo sat across from him, his face so wide open and hopeful that it hurt Liam's heart to look at him. "No matter what, I think you should do the show. Because Bill was like your dad *and* your mom, right? I mean, not your mom, but he was like your family. Like you are to me, now, right?" He ducked his head, looking suddenly bashful. Then he glanced up again. "And if Ballard Youth can help other kids like me, and if you're doing it for *him*, then maybe it's a good idea. It's okay to hope, right? For good things? Like, Brandy left, but you can still hope for happiness, yeah? Is that what you mean?"

The kid was smart. Wicked smart. "You *really* want to work on that show."

Timbo thumped backward dramatically in his chair. "*So bad.*"

"We'll see." Liam stuck the superhero's cape around his finger. "You might be right."

Timbo's eyebrows flew upward. "Oh, I'm *so* right."

Liam laughed and felt that hope again, right next to his heart. It felt dangerous. And good. He considered his Superman bandage. Felicia would be gone a few weeks. That was probably enough time for her company to come up with five more show ideas and start casting three of them.

But yeah. If Felicia actually turned out to be the buyer...

Liam shook his head to clear it. He finished making dinner.

They ate.

Timbo went upstairs to play Xbox.

Liam checked his email. There was one from Felicia.

We'd like to move ahead with the Maupin property. I'll be the buyer. If you and your brothers are amenable to the rest of the contract as-is, the network will remove the physical contact clause. Please move ahead with purchase negotiation. We'll start filming in three weeks.

That didn't give him much time. He assumed that they'd film walking through the other houses as if she were thinking about buying them, while she'd actually bought the treehouse. That timeline meant that within a month, provided the Maupin estate accepted their offer, Aidan could start the remodel. And given that the Maupin estate was managed by Mrs. Maupin's third cousin Dorene Hammer who'd always thought the redwood was unhappy about being hugged by a house with no way to get away (she was a poet), she'd accept.

Felicia's email was business-like. Terse and professional.

And just reading it, he imagined the smell of strawberry he'd caught on her skin while he'd kissed her, the scent of the Cat's Meow that had clung to her.

Strawberries had never been more erotic.

FIFTEEN

Twenty-two days later, Felicia drove back into Darling Bay in a graffiti-free rental car. She passed the wooden sign planted firmly in a well-tended patch of annuals. *Welcome to Darling Bay. Stay a While!*

This was real.

Imminent.

Her town.

She was buying the treehouse—the offer had been accepted and escrow had almost closed even though they'd film it like it hadn't already happened.

Soon she'd be part of Darling Bay, even as just a summer resident. Did they accept people like her? People who paid property taxes but only showed up for holidays? How long did it take to be known by the woman at the grocery store? By the bartender at the Golden Spike saloon?

She braked for an old man crossing the street with a walker. He was adorable, dressed in a black cowboy hat, black shirt and black jeans that looked two sizes too big for him. He glanced at her. Felicia sucked in a breath and waved.

And *he waved back.*

Felicia bit her bottom lip in delight.

Could this really be home? Someday? Every night in LA, she'd dreamed about walking the wooden floors of the Maupin house, climbing the redwood, sitting with her back pressed against the trunk, gazing out westward. Being inside the house, even for just those thirty minutes, had made her feel more at home than she'd ever thought she could feel. The fact that Liam had been standing next to her in the dreams held no meaning. Of course he was. He was the realtor.

Okay, and soon he would be her date.

Felicia *needed* the house. For that, she needed her job to be there waiting for her at the end of the show. That meant Liam was part of the network property, something to be wrangled and handled, exactly what Felicia was best at.

She parked in front of Ballard Brothers

Building and Realty. She took the steps up to Liam's office quickly and knocked before she lost her nerve. And as she waited, her heart rattled loosely in her chest, as if she hadn't put enough packing material around it. He'd been nothing but friendly in their email communications. Felicia and Natasha had had a Skype meeting regarding set load-in with all three brothers a week ago, and Liam had winked at them cheerily when they'd been logging off.

But the man had kissed her and had then literally hurled himself off a balcony to escape.

Felicia took a deep breath and knocked again. She touched the tangled wind chime. It *chunked* clumsily and went silent.

Timbo opened the door. He wore an oversized blue sweatshirt and his glasses were seated crookedly on his nose. He pulled the door open all the way and yelled over his shoulder, "Liam, she's here!" Then he brushed past her and bounced on the balls of his feet on the porch. "Just so you know, I'm still totally good with working on the show. Sorry, though, but I gotta go now."

"Big game?"

"Nah, that's this afternoon. This morning, me and the guys are going fishing."

"Where's your fishing pole?"

Timbo flashed her a smile, and she thought she could see the man he would grow into. "And by fishing, I mean wading in the creek that runs into the ocean." He ran down the steps and jumped on his bike. He was gone in a matter of seconds.

From behind Felicia, Liam spoke. "And by wading in the creek, he means watching the girls lay out."

"Boys'll be boys."

"Would you like some coffee?"

She held up both cups. "I'm supposed to ask *you* that. I got you an Americano at the Coffee Caboose."

He took it from her. "Was that just a good guess? Or did you ask someone?"

"I asked the blonde. Nikki? She said no cream, no sugar."

"There are no secrets in this town."

"There have to be some," she said lightly. "But they're probably only good ones. Want to go for a walk? Or can the network take you out to breakfast?"

"Look." Liam set the cup on the porch railing and jammed his hands into the pockets of his brown Dockers. "I shouldn't have kissed you. I was trying to make a point, and it was a stupid one."

"About the physical contact clause. I get it."

"I regret running away, though." He squinted at her. "I've never gone over a balcony to get away from a girl before."

Felicia felt the band around her forehead tighten. She was aimed at a headache if she didn't take a few deep breaths and get some more caffeine in her system. "Can you tell me what I did to make you do that? Because I have to admit, I sure felt like an idiot."

"I'm sorry. I overreacted. I wasn't used to the idea of the show yet."

Felicia chose to take that as a positive sign. "What can I do to make you more comfortable with the idea?"

"Maybe if you weren't yourself."

She choked on her drink.

Liam raised his hands. "That came out bad."

"Honest. It came out as honest." And hurtful. But Felicia was strong. Usually.

His words were hurried. "It's because I like you."

It was as though a boom mic had swung into her stomach. "Sorry?"

"You remember in fourth grade, when the boys all started pushing girls into the bushes? And pulling their hair and stealing their backpacks?"

Felicia nodded. "Donny Conner. I hated him."

"Yeah, well, he had a crush on you."

Instead of pain in her head, Felicia felt a peculiar lightheadedness. "He did?"

"He did. And so do I. But instead of pushing you into the bushes, I kissed you and then leaped over a wall to get away from you. My ex—that whole situation spooked me, I guess. And call me crazy, but I'm not excited to be put into a situation where I get paid for kissing someone I already want to kiss." He shook his head. "It's weird. It's Hollywood. Or maybe Vegas. Either way, I don't like it."

Felicia tried not to allow her feelings to be hurt *or* flattered.

He'd just said he wanted to kiss her. What if she just leaned forward? Right now? What if she tilted her head, and he...

No. Jesus. She was *working*.

She squashed the flips her stomach was doing. "I'm not your ex. I'm sorry for her dumping you, but I'd be trying to talk you into this no matter who the buyer was. That's my job, and it's my own damn fault I've made it so much more difficult by wanting to be the person buying the house my boss wants to feature on the first episode. And I'll level with you. We do want to use you to make money for us. But if we make money, you make money. And I can assure you that I'll keep being honest with you. I'll tell you if I think I can get you more money, more perks, more anything, I'll let you know."

"We're still interested in the money."

In the money. Not in her.

That was fine. Totally fine. Better that way. "I got the physical contact clause taken out. I'm still surprised. I didn't think Natasha *would* agree to it."

"How did you get her to?"

It had taken Felicia twenty minutes. In the six years she'd been working for the woman, they'd never had a conversation on one topic for twenty minutes, ever. Natasha made up her mind in seconds. She gave decrees, and they were followed. She was the brains behind every blockbuster show the network had, and she had the most power a person could have in Hollywood. *No one* argued with her for twenty full minutes.

But Felicia had. "I told her that the longer we run the show without you guys falling in love, the better." Technically, if each man fell in love right off the bat, the show might be played out in three successful episodes. The working title of the show was *On the Market*. It made sense to keep at least a couple of the guys on the market for as long as it took.

"I would have thought that would be obvious."

"Look, you know this stuff is often pretty scripted, right?"

"I know almost nothing about this, but yeah, that doesn't surprise me."

"Natasha had originally planned on having a home run on the first episode."

The planes of his face lengthened as his jaw dropped. "She was planning on making me fall for whatever woman they picked? Or she was just going to make it look like that?"

Sheepish. That was what this feeling was. Felicia was used to feeling proud to be in the television industry. She wasn't used to feeling embarrassed about it. "It's amazing what they can do in post-production editing."

"Wow." He glanced out at the street and waved at a redheaded woman pushing a stroller. "Just wow."

"I know."

"And soon you'll have a house in Darling Bay."

The words—or was it his voice?—made her shiver. "Oh, my god. Yeah. I will." A house here. In this town.

Near *this* man with the light blue eyes and the mouth that was made for kissing her.

Liam had apparently pounded his coffee. He crushed the empty cup like a beer can and perched it on the railing. "Okay, then. What next?"

Relief washed through her body, making her

knees feel loose. "We tell the camera crew to meet us at the house. And we start filming."

"Today? They're here in town?"

"Flying in right now. Should be here in an hour, which gives us just enough time."

"You were that sure?"

She shook her head. "I wasn't. Natasha was."

SIXTEEN

Liam had made it a point not to regret things in his life. Their mother had regretted having children—Liam had heard her say it, just before she left. She didn't mean for him to hear, but he had, and he'd told himself he wouldn't regret a damn thing when he grew up. If he screwed up, he apologized. If he made a wrong choice, he just lived with it and decided differently next time.

But Liam was already regretting saying yes to the show, and the cameras had been rolling for less than a minute.

"So, Liam." Felicia's hands rested on her hips, and she gazed up at the Maupin house from the driveway below. "What can you tell me about this property?"

They were supposed to act like they'd never been here before. Felicia was supposed to fall in love with it all over again "for the first time" while the crew filmed. And she was doing a great job. She'd said this same sentence at least seven times already.

Every time Liam tried to get any words out, they got stuck in his throat.

Or the sentences came out in the wrong order.

Or his voice just didn't plain work.

This was hell, and they weren't even in the house yet.

He opened his mouth and said, "Well, Felindasha. Aw, *shit.*"

The guy who'd wired their clothing mics snorted.

"People get my name wrong all the time, but that's a new one."

"I can't do this." He hadn't felt this stupid since the time he bounced a check for his own mortgage because he moved money into the wrong account. "I'm sorry. I just don't think I'm going to get this."

"You'll get used to the cameras. Here's what I suggest. We skip this part. It's clearly making you a little nervous. Let's head up the hill, and go into the house. Inside, they'll be focusing on me, not you, and we can just come back and film this part later."

"I thought there would be more time. Like,

they'd make me learn lines. Or they'd put me in new clothing, make me cut my hair or something. I'm just surprised by all this." He gestured at the two full camera crews, the three dollies which didn't seem to like rolling through dirt at all. "And that." He pointed at the four trailers that had pulled up the rutted driveway. He'd been told one held the canteen, and the others housed post-production. "This is crazy."

"It can be overwhelming, I know."

No wonder Felicia was good at her job. Her smile, so warm and open, made him feel like everything was going to be okay, and Liam knew it was *not*. He would never be able to do this. "How is this happening so quickly? I thought it would take months."

"The network is known for grab-n-go. Natasha had an idea at three in the morning once and we were shooting it that afternoon."

"How did that go?" *Come on, say that it crashed and burned.*

"That became *Remaindered*."

"Holy crap." He didn't watch TV, but he knew about that one, where famous authors had to hand sell their own books at flea markets. The ones who remained undercover the longest won the chance at their books being optioned for a blockbuster movie.

"She's good at what she does." Felicia looked up

at the house, and a pink glow lit her cheeks. "Want to go inside?"

She couldn't hide her excitement—she was practically radiating it like heat from the old woodstove in his house and she was cute as hell. "Sure."

"Oh, *good*. Guys?"

Even the way the camera handlers—she'd told him what they were called, but he had only remembered their names, Tony and Gene—spoke to her told him she was respected. They wanted to please her.

One camera went inside to film her "first reaction" to seeing the inside of the house. Another stayed behind Liam, and a woman watching a small handheld monitor trailed behind all of them.

It would be good if Liam could say something simple on the doorstep. Something like, "You ready?" Or even, "Let's take a look."

But when the wide-angle camera swung back to him, all he could do was throw a crooked smile in Felicia's direction. He probably looked drunk. Lord knew he felt wobbly enough when she smiled at him.

If this worked, if this actually went onto TV and they paid him and his brothers, he'd be watched by millions.

Or rather, millions would watch him watch Felicia.

Because that's all he really felt like doing, after all. Her hair was doing that thing women's hair on television did, hanging in long, heavy-looking waves down to the middle of her back. The only hair and makeup for him was a swipe of powder from a woman wearing an apron full of brushes. He'd seen her try to put more on Felicia, but after a dusting of powder, Felicia had waved the woman away, slicking on her own red lipstick instead.

Now, behind Felicia, he regretted not being able to speak English anymore, but he was glad for the fact that he had to follow her into the house. It meant he could stare at her ass in those jeans that were snug in all the right places.

She shot a look over her shoulder at him and then swung open the arched door. "I'm nervous."

"Don't be." His first non-garbled words. "You're going to love this."

Inside, the camera pulled back as she entered the kitchen.

She looked at him, and then at the kitchen. Then back at him. "Oh, god." She covered her mouth. "I don't know what to say."

SEVENTEEN

Felicia wasn't kidding. She'd lost all her words, just by entering the house that made her feel so welcome she wanted to lie down and hug the floor with wide-spread arms.

She turned into Liam, outside. "This..." The wide, dark beams overhead caught her eye. "Oh, this is just—"

"Pretty special, isn't it?"

Liam sounded like a pro. He leaned on a dark wood hutch that looked as if it had been built into place. In fact, *he* looked like he'd come with the house. She hadn't noticed outside, but the shirt he was wearing, light blue chambray with Western pockets, looked as vintage as the wood he leaned on. He must have shaved, but his stubble was coming in fast. All he needed was a cowboy hat, and the kitchen would turn into something from the Old West.

"It's...it's, um." Stage fright? She had no idea if she had it or not. She'd never tried being on this side of the lens. And outside, talking to Liam when he couldn't scrape together a sensible syllable, she hadn't been nervous at all. But in here, it *mattered* so much more.

Liam's eyes showed her mercy. "All of the wood in the house is the same as the tree that grows in the middle. Redwood is plentiful, and because of the tannins that give it its beautiful color, it actually doesn't have to be chemically treated for insects, decay, or fire. Come on through to the parlor. I can't wait to show you how the tree forms a wall near the stairs."

He was suddenly perfect. A natural.

Felicia nodded at him so hard her neck hurt. What the hell was wrong with her?

Tony on Camera 2 walked quietly backward, focused on Liam, and Gene followed behind her. Her heart beat so hard it felt like it was taking up all the blood in her body—her hands were numb and tingly. She had better not faint. It would do great for ratings, but she wasn't quite ready to sacrifice her body for the network.

Liam pulled back long curtains in the parlor to

let in sunshine. "It needs a little TLC." He patted the back of an old chaise, and she coughed as a small dust storm rose. He batted at the air, as if his hands could clear it. "It'll take some work. And I'm no contractor—that's the part my brothers do. But just imagine it with a new floor. Parquet, maybe?"

She looked down. The floor's wooden slats were old, scuffed in places, gleaming in others. It was obviously original. She didn't want a new floor, she wanted to skate over these exact floors in socks in winter, and glide over them barefoot in summer. She wanted to *feel* the house.

But what she managed to say was, "Yum."

Yum?

Gene leaned his head out from behind the camera to stare at her. Liam straight up laughed.

"I'm sorry." She made a throat cutting motion. "Quit rolling. This isn't working."

Tony pushed a button and the red lights went off. "Damn, Felicia. This is all still hand-held. What are you going to do when the rolling dollies get in here?"

"I'm not an actress, am I?"

Anna, the production manager standing in for Felicia, sighed. "This is supposed to be both spontaneous and unscripted. What could possibly be easier than that? You talk like normal people. Liam can't do it outside, and you can't do it in here. I do *not* get it."

A line of sweat dripped down the center of Felicia's back. That would make a nice visual onscreen if the camera followed her anywhere. More of the same sweat, now cold and clammy, coated the palms of her hands. "I'm sorry, but I'm freaking out. I need five."

"Fine." Anna crooked a finger at a PA who looked as nervous as Felicia felt. "Outside. We'll work on set-up shots." She pointed the same finger first at Liam, then at Felicia. "You two. Talk. Work it out."

Felicia said, "Wait. Leave me the two handhelds."

Anna snorted. "Really?"

Felicia arched an eyebrow. She was the one on screen, yes, but she was also Anna's boss. "Come back in fifteen minutes."

Anna grumbled but left the Go-Pro cameras on a low coffee table and left.

Liam picked up one of the tiny cameras and pointed it in her direction. "Say cheese."

Yes. Maybe this would work. "Exactly. Turn that on."

"Yeah?"

"Can't hurt to try."

The red light glowed. "So, Felicia. I'm dying to know what you think about this place. Honestly."

She thumped down into a dark green couch. Dust rose in an identical storm to the first, and right on cue, she sneezed. "I love it."

"I knew you would. Tell me what you love?"

She wasn't nervous anymore. "I love this furniture."

Liam panned away from her, filming the large room and its ancient sofas and chairs, before coming back to her. "This stuff went out of style a million years ago. We can talk the seller down for getting rid of it."

Felicia kicked off her shoes and crossed her legs underneath her. "If by getting rid of it you mean making this sofa the focus piece of the room, then yes. It needs to be cleaned, but it's the most comfortable thing I've ever sat on."

"Seriously?" He looked over the camera display at her in obvious surprise.

She patted the space next to her. "You have to try it."

Liam sat. "Oh, man. You ain't kidding."

She reached for the camera and pointed it at him. "What would it take for me to get these pieces cleaned?"

"Talia Moorhead in town runs the antique shop. She does reupholstery. I can talk her into it."

Something softened in his face, and Felicia wanted to lower the phone-sized camera, but she didn't. "You love this place. Darling Bay, I mean. Why?"

"It's home. It's where I'm from."

"I'm from Reseda. I don't love it."

"This is where my people are."

"Your brothers."

He nodded. "Yeah. The knuckleheads I share DNA with. I love those guys."

Felicia zoomed in to a close-up on his face. Women would die, watching him talk about his family. He was the real deal. He'd look just as good blown up poster-size as he did in the little camera screen.

"But it's more than just them. I love the Golden Spike and the way you can get a free song on the jukebox if you jiggle the cord when Nate's not looking. I love that Dot Rillo at the post office rations the new stamps when they're first released—until Mark Wong comes in to buy his, no one else in town gets them."

"Why Mark Wong?"

"He's forty-five and has Downs Syndrome." Liam grinned, and his smile blazed at her. "He's the most excited philatelist you'll ever meet in your life. He eats, breaths, and sleeps stamps. He was the first person in town to get the upside-down two-dollar reprint of the Flying Jenny, and he said in the newspaper it was the happiest day of his life."

"I want to meet him."

Liam tilted his head. "Are you serious about wanting to live here? In Darling Bay?" He took the camera and focused it back on her. Instead of making her nervous, the intensity with which he was looking at her over the lens made her feel more confident.

"I've never felt like this about a place before." Felicia knew the editors would use this, would make it look like they were having this conversation after she'd seen the whole place, which, of course, she already had. "It feels like the place I was meant to be."

"What else do you love about it?"

She wrinkled her nose. "The smell. It smells like a forest, and not in a Pine-Sol kind of way. It smells like we're in the woods, as if the house is still growing around us."

"In a very real way, the center of the house still *is* growing."

"The heart of it." She turned to face him and stretched out her legs. Without asking—without really thinking anything at all—she slid her bare feet under his thigh. It felt like the right place for her to be. Right there, next to him. "The heart of the house is getting bigger every day."

"I love that. What else?"

"I love these floors, the ones you want to rip up."

"My brother Aidan will have some fantastic ideas when we get him in here. Maybe some old-growth reclaimed lumber, sanded and smoothed to perfection?"

"No." She grinned. "And before you say anything else, I want to keep this rug."

Liam swung the camera to the stag-hunting scene on the floor. "It has holes, you know."

"I can repair it." They were doing it. They were repeating what they'd said on the first time through, but letting it sound natural at the same time.

"You're a tapestry weaver now?"

"I've never tried." Felicia held up her fingers and waggled them. His thigh was reassuringly heavy and warm on the tops of her feet. "But I bet Talia-whats-her-name at the antique shop knows someone who can teach me?"

"Bet she does."

Then, in a move she couldn't have scripted, Liam caught her hand with his free one. "What do you think about the town itself?"

Felicia swallowed the frog that rose in her throat. She was suddenly nervous again and it had nothing to do with the tiny camera Liam still pointed at her and everything to do with the warmth of his fingers. "I don't know anything about Darling Bay, not really. I've seen the inside of my bed and breakfast, and I can tell you that if you're looking for stuffed animals that make noise, the Cat's Meow has all of them. The world's supply of fake meowing cats is inside those walls."

"Want to go on a date with me?" His fingers tangled in hers, warm and dry.

Her stomach flipped. That was the whole point of this—dating a Ballard brother while the others fixed up the place. And Liam was capturing it—getting her on camera, just as he should. But crap, *he* wasn't being filmed. "Hang on. We have to catch you right now, too."

"I ask you out and this is what you say?" But he didn't sound put out. He filmed her as she pulled her feet out from under him. She stood and moved a tall chair to her side of the couch. She propped the second camera on it, made sure it was on and that Liam was in the center of the screen.

Then she took another chair and set it next to him. "I'll take that, thank you, sir." She aimed the camera at where she'd been sitting. "It'll autofocus."

"So we really have to run through this again?"

She grinned and sat. She tucked her feet under his thigh again. "This still okay?"

He nodded and reached for her hand. "Is this?"

Felicia nodded. Something hung in the air between them, a thickness that felt soft on her skin, an electric current that was humming at just the places that touched. Her feet tingled. Her fingers could have shot sparks.

"So." She cleared her throat. "Can we try that again?"

His blue eyes sparkled. "Want to go on a date with me?"

Felicia nodded. "Yes. Yes, okay. Yeah." Great, was she going to start sounding dumb again? "Yes. Where should we go?"

His eyebrows rose. "Darling Bay. Obviously."

EIGHTEEN

Felicia had been sure he'd understood how it worked, but maybe he was having her say it for the sake of the audience? Smart guy. She was impressed all over again. "No, no. We can go anywhere."

He just kept those light blue eyes on hers. She wanted to get closer to them, to study them, to see if those gold flecks were she saw in their depths were tricks of the light.

But he was quiet, so she elaborated more. "*Anywhere* we want. The only thing we have to do is agree on the location. Have you ever been to Paris?"

"No, ma'am."

Was he drawling on purpose? If so, she loved it. She squeezed his fingers. This was going to play *so* well on screen. "Or Venice. We could take an overnight flight once your brothers start work on the house and cruise the canals in style. You haven't lived until you've danced in St. Mark's Square to an open-air band."

"Guess I haven't lived, then."

"What about Fiji? We could get one of those cabanas that sit right over the water."

"But we have the same exact ocean. Right out there. Why take that long a flight, when we've got everything we need right here?"

He really was making her work, wasn't he? "Okay. Melbourne?"

"Scary insects that bite."

"Thailand?"

"Tsunamis." His thumb caressed the back of her hand. Goosebumps rose on her skin, and she wondered if he could feel them.

"What's preventing a tsunami from rolling in here?"

"I know where the high ground is here. I don't know about Thailand." He shifted to face her more and drew her hand nearer to him as a result. "I don't mean to sound like a bumpkin. I have a passport, and I'll go somewhere someday. But on a date with you? I want to stay in Darling Bay."

Felicia decided to not think about the cameras. Whatever she did wrong, they could fix in editing. "No, seriously, Liam. Money isn't a problem. They'll literally send us anywhere. We can't go into space, but that's just about where the line is."

"Are you really serious about buying this house?"

She nodded.

"And you said you don't know anything about Darling Bay."

"That's right, but —"

"Then I want to show you. I bet you didn't know that when the sun sets, there's a little crowd of old people who gather to clap every night."

"You're kidding."

"I'm not. I used to think it was kind of dumb, but then I was walking past one evening and I decided to join them. I gotta say, there's something pretty damn awesome about applauding for the sun putting on a show. And then there's the folly at Stine's Cove. And the pier! You haven't walked on the pier yet. You haven't met Ethel, Parrot Freddy's bird, and you haven't seen what the Rayburn brothers do to new graves at the cemetery."

He made it—all of it— sound amazing. But she had to be clear. "Not London? Not Bombay?"

In answer, he lifted her hand to his lips, and kissed the tip of her index finger. It was the lightest touch, barely a breath, but it seemed to suck the air right out of Felicia's lungs.

"I really want to kiss you." Liam's voice was hoarse. "But I keep thinking about the cameras."

"We'll both have to work on getting less camera shy." Felicia felt bold, and then bolder as she saw his eyes go darker as he kissed the tip of her middle finger. Then he kissed his way across her palm, and by the time he reached her wrist, she was liquid inside. He set his camera on the floor.

She moved fast and dropped her camera to the sofa next to her. She pulled her hand back bringing his with hers. Then somehow, without knowing how she got there, her mouth was a breath away from his. For one long second, they stayed there, separated by only the heat of their gaze.

Felicia kissed him.

And lord, if he didn't kiss her back. His mouth was hot, his lips fierce. Her tongue grazed his. He tasted faintly of mint and strongly of desire. She twisted, and he moved with her. She was in his lap, then, and she could feel how aroused he had become. The kiss lasted forever, and that forever was only a scrap of time. She felt like she could kiss him for the next five years, and she wouldn't need a break. She wouldn't need sleep or water or food.

She would just need *him*, the way his mouth fit hers, the way his hand slid behind her neck and tangled in her hair, drawing her deeper into the kiss, into him, into exactly where she wanted to be.

The temperature in the room soared to approximately a thousand degrees, and if they hadn't been in the middle of trying to film an episode, Felicia would have been tempted to lift her shirt, to take off his, to reach for his belt—right there, where any of her coworkers could stumble upon them.

Her coworkers. Oh, shit.

She pulled back. His breathing was ragged, but hers was even more so. She touched her bottom lip, feeling the grazed skin his stubble had left behind. "We have to..."

"I know."

Carefully, she slid sideways and turned her body so that she was sitting next to him, her thigh pressed against his. She breathed through her mouth as slowly as she could, attempting to pretend that he didn't make her feel as crazy as he did.

It was almost impossible.

Liam moved to touch her hand, and then as if thinking better of it, stopped. "You scare me a little."

"Why?" Her voice didn't sound like her own. It was rough, and low.

"You make me want to tell the truth."

"And you usually lie?"

He shook his head. "No. You make me want to trust that you are who you seem to be." He leaned his head back against the sofa and rubbed his eyes. "And that makes me nervous."

"Who do I seem to be?"

"A woman who isn't afraid of living. Of feeling."

Felicia couldn't help it. She laughed. "You're the first person who's ever said that to me, I can promise you."

"Sorry?"

She inched away from him so that they weren't touching. "Everyone I've ever known has told me I need to watch less TV, to get out in the world and live. I fired a therapist over it, actually." Had she ever sounded more Los Angeles? "Oh, my god, I don't know why I'm telling you this."

"You produce shows about love. Or as close to love as television can get. I'd wager your feelings are pretty close to the surface."

She dug her nails into the palms of her hands. "We should probably wrap this up and go find the others."

"Oh, yeah? That does touch a nerve, huh?"

"We have a lot to do." She stood, smoothing non-existing wrinkles in her jeans. "I'm thinking that I want this room to stay very much like it is, I've already said that, but I need to meet with Aidan and talk about what we're going to do with the bathroom, and the upstairs room. I need to schedule that with him. And Jake—I need him, too." What she didn't need was Liam's eyes on her. "This is a whirlwind shoot—are you really sure your brothers can get it done in a few days?"

He stayed seated, as if he had all the time in the world, which maybe he did. But Felicia didn't. She now had two full-time jobs, being on the show as well as producing it (somehow, the fake "firing" hadn't come through, even though she'd signed the cash bonus paperwork). Somewhere in there, she had to go on a filmed date with a man who made her more nervous than anyone possibly ever had.

"They can do anything if they can afford to hire the right crew."

"The money isn't a problem." She wanted her purse, wanted to dig out a mint and pop it, to get rid of the taste of him.

"Felicia. I'm sorry. I didn't mean to push you."

Without stopping to think whether it was the right or wrong thing to say, Felicia spoke. "I don't actually *like* feeling my feelings. Feelings are stupid. They hurt, and they're messy, and I like tidy. I like neat. I like being able to put things in boxes, and I like being able to categorize things. Maybe that's why I like television. Everything is always wrapped up, if not by the end of the hour, then by the end of the season. That's important to me. Feelings, whether they're good or bad, whether they're upset or excited or in love, don't fit into boxes. So, no. If you see me as a person who feels her feelings, you're not seeing me at all."

"I see you." His face was open, his posture relaxed with his arms resting at his sides.

"I'm just going to check on a couple of things with Anna. I'll be back in a minute." She put on a smile she didn't feel and she walked out of the parlor.

He didn't follow her.

In the kitchen, Anna and Tony were arguing about the best place to set up the diary cams.

Felicia had no idea why she'd been so honest with Liam.

She wished to hell she hadn't been. It was just going to make everything harder.

NINETEEN

The diary cam had shaken him up.

He hadn't expected it to, though he should have. "Keep a video diary" had been mentioned in the contract, but he kind of assumed it would be Felicia talking to it. She was the buyer, after all.

So when Anna asked him to sit the kitchen with her, and speak into the camera she'd set up next to the stove, he was tense. "I still don't know how this is a diary if you're here, or why you want it from me."

Anna, a young woman with bright orange glasses that matched both her orange nose ring and her orange lipstick, smiled at him. She looked tired. "We film a lot. We get as many hours as we can, and then we'll strip it all back into a forty-eight minute show. The more we have in the can, the more choices we have. And as for the diary part, I'll feed you a few questions. Just look into the camera and respond in full sentences, as if you're just thinking about these things."

Liam settled himself on the stool. "This seems pretty damn fake."

"Welcome to Hollywood."

Anna asked him innocuous questions at first, things about what he did at his job, what he liked about Darling Bay. She asked him what his brothers did, and that was easy, of course. Aidan built things. Jake did whatever the hell he wanted, but was good at helping Aidan out. Liam was good with paperwork. He grimaced into the camera. "See? Boring as cement drying."

"Which one are you closest to?"

"I'm closest to whichever one isn't actively being a pain in my ass."

"What was your last relationship like?"

"Heartbreaking."

Anna shook her head. "Remember, phrase it as a full sentence."

This was *so* dumb. "I guess you would say my last relationship was heartbreaking. And it was. My heart broke when she didn't show up for the wedding rehearsal. But then I got over it."

Anna blew out a breath. She looked as frustrated as he felt. "Okay, let's try another one."

Liam didn't want to do this anymore. He wanted to go home and hang out with Timbo on the couch and eat pizza and yell at the ball game together. But Timbo had a youth group meeting that night—a sleep-over at the school—and pizza wasn't as fun alone.

"Liam, I need you to be open. Candid."

"Why?"

"Because authenticity will make you interesting, and if you're interesting, people tune in. It's a simple formula."

"I thought this whole thing was about being fake."

"Common misperception. Okay, what do you fear the most? Answer quickly in a complete sentence, please." Anna pushed a button on the camera and looked away as if she were disinterested.

What did he fear the most? Honestly?

Fine. What the hell did he have to lose? The whole town already knew about Brandy ditching him, and he didn't care what the rest of the world thought, anyway. "I guess when my ex dumped me, she confirmed the worst. I'd always kind of been convinced I'd never get married. That I'd never find the one." He paused. The camera lens still made him nervous.

What if it was Felicia sitting there, looking at him with those big brown eyes? Just imagining her made him feel more comfortable, instantly. "I've always thought I was unlovable, since I was a kid, since my parents—anyway. Brandy proved it to me, that if I showed my real self to someone, they'd leave. I guess my biggest fear is that I'll never figure out how to *be* lovable." As soon as the words were out, he felt a little sick.

It wasn't Felicia he was talking to. It was the whole world.

He stood, astonished that someone telling him to be honest and then not looking at him had actually worked. It was a dirty trick. "And that is maybe the worst thing I've ever said out loud, and I want to take it back. How do I get you not to put that on the show?"

"Nah, it's fine." Anna scratched notes on a piece of paper. She didn't look at him.

"It's *not* fine. I don't agree to that being aired."

"Talk to Felicia, then. That's the producer's call, not mine."

Shit.

TWENTY

Liam took his best guess, and ordered the pizza half Hawaiian, half everything. At the store, Martha had let him buy a six-pack of mixed beers, so Felicia would have a choice from light and hoppy to dark and bitter.

Feelings. She was right, they were stupid. They got in the way of everything.

The problem was, you couldn't get away from them, no matter how you tried. And Liam had tried.

Felicia had given him her cell phone number earlier, when she'd left the house. "In case you need anything." Her voice had been all business, her smile bright. And fake.

Now, parked in front of the bed and breakfast, he texted her. *Have you eaten?*

He waited, watching the door at her balcony. The night was shockingly cold, but that was par for Darling Bay's course. Hot summer days led to thicker than normal fog banks. When they rolled in, they brought the ocean wind. Inland, it stayed warm, but right on the coast it could drop to the low fifties inside an hour. He pulled the zipper of his sweatshirt higher.

And he waited.

Five minutes later, he texted again. *Because I'm parked in front. I have pizza and beer.*

There was no motion yet.

I did one of those diary cams. This is a bribe so it doesn't air.

The curtain of her room twitched. He waved though he couldn't see her.

Then the balcony door opened, and Felicia came out.

He got out of the car and waved again.

Felicia's expression was lighter than it had been when she'd left the treehouse. Her mouth was more relaxed, and her hair was pulled into a ponytail. She leaned on her forearms as he came to stand below, on the edge of the garden which was so thickly planted with flowers it resembled a parade float. "This isn't necessary."

"Did you already eat?"

She shook her head.

Though he'd imagined them eating in her strawberry-scented room, he had a better idea. "Let's have a picnic."

"Where?"

"The house."

"The crew…"

"They'll be gone by now for the night, won't they?"

She blinked down at him. Had she been napping? One side of her face was red, as if she'd been lying on it. "Maybe."

"Come on. Eat pizza with me. I'll drive."

Felicia squinted. "I want my car with me."

"Then meet me there." Risking it, he turned to walk back to his car.

"What did you say on the diary cam?"

Over his shoulder, he said, "I'll tell you over dinner!"

He heard her balcony door close, and all he could do was hope she'd follow.

At the treehouse, it looked as if the crew had left—all their cars were gone, and the trailer parked to the right of the old garden was dark. The wind sighed in the oak trees, but everything else was quiet.

He waited, leaning against his car.

Three minutes behind him, her rental car crunched gravel as it came up the dirt driveway.

The wind caught strands of her ponytail, throwing them in her eyes. "It's cold out here." She pushed her hair back.

"Then we go inside. We'll get some pizza in you, and then you'll feel better."

"Feelings are stupid," she said lightly. "But we can try it."

Liam led the way inside, his heart clattering in his chest. He was nervous. It was silly, and he felt fourteen years old and stupid, but he liked it. "Where do you want to eat? Dining room? Kitchen? Up in the treehouse's treehouse?"

She shook her head. "Too cold. I feel like I have a chill in my bones. In the parlor? Is that okay?"

"Of course it is."

In the parlor, he put the pizza box on the long, low table in front of the dark green sofa they'd sat on before, the one she loved. "Here we go."

She sat, her movements stiff.

Liam took off his jacket. "Want to wear this?"

"Come on." She smiled, but it didn't reach her eyes. "The cameras aren't on. You don't have to try to be amazing."

"Try? It just comes natural." He draped the jacket around her shoulders. "Just wear it for a minute. You'll warm up." He opened the pizza box. "This'll help, too."

She took a slice.

He did the same.

God, this was awkward. What the hell had he been thinking? He *should* have just eaten at home, alone, while Timbo spent the night as his sleep-over. He could have had three beers on the couch and fallen asleep to the sound of the news.

Felicia used her slice to point at the pink mantelpiece. "I wonder if the fireplace works."

"The inspection came back clear on it, but I'd get a sweep out here to check it before you light a fire."

"I've always wanted to live in a house with a real fireplace."

"As opposed to..."

"The gas kind. Like I have in my condo. It seems like cheating." She pulled an olive off her slice and popped it in her mouth. "I wish we could light it right now."

"We'll just pretend it's burning."

"Pretend." Her voice was dull. "Sure."

"You don't like pretend? Seems to me like lots of folks prefer it."

"What do you mean?"

Liam pushed the six pack closer to her and chose one of the two IPAs for himself. "My whole business, sometimes. People tell themselves what they want to buy, where they want to live, but really what they're talking about is who they want to pretend they are. They think with a bigger house, they'll be more important. Or with a better kitchen, they think they'll be a better cook. But it's all just pretend. They walk into their new houses the exact same people who locked the door behind them at the last house."

Felicia chose a bottle of the dark beer. "So we both deal in lies."

She was distractingly beautiful. She had no makeup on, her lips chewed clean of lipstick. Her hair was caught back in that ponytail, strands of it hanging loose. She was wearing what looked like black yoga pants and his jacket, and to him, she looked perfect.

What had she just said? Lies.

That wasn't it, not exactly. Liam took a sip of his beer as he thought. "Maybe we both deal in hope. Fantasies. The people who watch your shows hope that they can someday have lives like the ones they see. And the people I work with who move from house to house are hoping that they'll find what they're looking for."

"That's a nice way of putting it. I guess that a lot of people who watch our shows just want to escape their own lives and dream of something different."

They chewed their way through two slices of pizza each. The silence wasn't exactly companionable, but it wasn't as awkward as it felt at the start.

As they picked up their third sizes, Liam said, "Your girl Anna grilled me today after you left."

"She's good at that. I trained her myself. The diary cam?"

"She asked me what my biggest fear was."

"Oooh, that's one of my favorites. What did you say?"

"That's the problem. I was too truthful. I don't want it to be aired in the show." Liam felt a tightness in his chest.

"Let's talk about it." She sounded like she was speaking from a script. "I'm sure we can work something out."

"And I don't want *you* to look at the footage."

"What, are you a serial killer? Because if it you are, we should pay you even more than we already are. You'd kill in the ratings." She paused. "Get it?"

"Come on." He thought about taking another bite of pizza, but his stomach was suddenly tense.

"It can't be that bad."

"It's not. It's just really personal."

Her eyes lit up, as if he'd said something that pleased her. Perfect. The more embarrassed he was, the more money her show would make? No. That wasn't right. "Come on, how would you feel?"

"What?" She carefully placed her slice back on the paper plate.

"You tell me yours." Liam was suddenly sure this was the right thing to say. "Your biggest fear."

TWENTY-ONE

A pause. "I think I already did."

Liam shook his head. He wasn't going to let her off that easily. "You're going to have to be more specific than that."

She heaved a long sigh and slid off the couch to the rug. She dropped backward dramatically and stared at the ceiling. "That whole..."

"Yeah?"

Felicia turned her head and looked at him. "No."

"What?"

"I told you already. If you didn't hear then, I don't need to repeat it."

"Your biggest fear is that you can't handle real

feelings?" That was nothing. Everyone felt that way.

She didn't answer— she just kept her eyes on his.

He shifted his weight on the sofa, wanting to lie on the floor next to her but feeling it might scare her. "What about nuclear war? What about plague? Or locusts? Or a plague of locusts?"

"Those are just things to worry about in the middle of the night. I can't do anything about them. Feelings are something I should be able to *do* something about."

"I wish feelings worked that way." His didn't, anyway. They were messy. Part of being human.

"Will you tell me what you said in the diary? Please?"

"You'll take it out? If I tell you?"

For a long moment, Felicia was silent. Her eyes stayed on his, and he felt a hollow in the middle of his abdomen, an emptiness that food couldn't fill.

Finally, she turned onto her side so that she faced him and propped her head on her hand. "Okay, I'll keep it out."

"Really?"

"If you tell me what you said. Then yes. Natasha won't see it."

Oh, god.

But why the hell not? After all, he'd pretended

he'd been speaking to her when he said it. "I have this dumb fear about people leaving me. That they won't think I'm lovable enough to stay."

"Go on."

He grimaced. "Do I have to?"

"Is this about the last girlfriend?"

"Brandy? I suppose so, that's why it came up, but that's not what it's about."

She stayed silent and kept her gaze on his. She nodded, and that was all he needed to know, that she was with him.

"Everyone knows our parents left, first my dad, then a few years later, my mom. But no one knows why. No one knows why our step-dad Bill kept us after my mom was gone. Except for me."

"What happened?"

God help him. He wanted to tell her. "Before they split up, I heard my parents arguing. My dad thought they could make more money cooking if they went south, into the valley."

"He was a cook?"

"Yeah, not like that. They cooked meth. One my first memories is my mother bundling us out of the house as fast as she could go, my dad screaming at her that it was safe. It didn't blow up, but it could have."

"That's terrible."

"That's not even the bad part. My mom

wouldn't go south with him because he said he'd only take Aidan."

He watched it register in her eyes. "Not you. Or Jake."

Liam nodded. "He left, and she got as clean as she could. Everyone thinks that Bill married my mom because he loved her, but that was never true, at least in the romantic sense. He'd been born gay, but that was a different time. He hadn't come out yet, and they were good friends. The marriage helped both of them. She let him adopt us, and she was his beard for a while."

"But this is California."

He shrugged. "Darling Bay was a small town. It was different here in the eighties. It worked for them. Then she met a guy who got her hooked again."

"Oh, Liam." She reached out and touched his wrist lightly.

"My brothers were always outside, building something, falling off what they built, breaking limbs, making flying machines. I hung out with them sometimes, but I'd gotten pretty used to watching my parents, to making sure that they didn't fall asleep and hurt themselves. So I was the kid with the book, reading somewhere close by. No one ever noticed me. That's why I was the one lucky enough to be privy to the fight my mom and

Bill had, right before she left. She wanted to take Jake with her. Just Jake."

"But...not Aidan? And I don't get it. Why not *you*?"

That was the question he'd been trying to answer his whole life. "Bill threatened to have her arrested for child abandonment if she left us behind, said that he'd have the courts give all of us to him permanently. She fled then, leaving all of us."

Felicia moved quickly, sitting up and crossing her legs. She leaned forward. "That's *awful*."

"It was. I think it broke Bill's heart in a lot of ways. He'd married her in order to help her. He loved her in his way. He got good and drunk for a while, until one night I pointed out that if he kept drinking that hard, he'd lose all three of us, too." The memory came back then, the image as clear as if it had happened last week. Bill, sitting in that small yellow kitchen, his eyes red with both tears and anger. *What about you, boy? How the hell do two parents just forget about a kid like you?* Bill had hugged him tightly and sent him to bed. "He told me I mattered, too. The next morning, he was sober and he stayed that way till the day he died."

"It sounds like you made a difference to him. Like he loved you."

"Yeah." Liam twisted a cheese packet. "He did

love us. All of us. So hell. I don't know what my damn problem is."

"Well, Bill died, which is a kind of abandonment, right? Your dad didn't choose you, and your mom didn't choose you, either. Those were the two people who were supposed to choose you the hardest. Sounds pretty obvious to me. When Brandy left, it must have felt just like that."

A thick knot rose in Liam's throat, but it wasn't about Brandy. It was about the way Felicia was listening to him. "Sure."

"What actually happened to your parents?"

"My mom went back to my dad, and while they were sleeping, their lab exploded. The firefighters said they wouldn't have felt a thing." One of Liam's most shameful memories was hearing the fire captain say that to him, and wishing that maybe they'd felt it a little. Maybe just a tiny little bit.

"Holy shit. I'm so sorry."

"Anyway." He took a breath. "I never told my brothers I heard them say that. Aidan doesn't know our mom didn't want him, and Jake doesn't know our dad would have left him behind. And neither of them need to know I'd have been chosen by no one. They're loyal to a fault. It would hurt them too much."

"Loyalty's a wonderful trait."

The knot in his throat eased. "Yeah. Anyway, I

guess that's why we're all so involved with at-risk youth. The money that we're making from the show, all of it, will go into finally opening Ballard Youth, an after-school program that we've been trying to make happen for years."

Felicia nodded. "That's why you have Timbo."

"His mom chose meth over him, too."

"I don't *understand* that."

"Normal people, non-addicts, don't." He picked up his beer and slid off the sofa so that they were both sitting on the rug. "What were your parents like?"

Felicia hugged her bent legs. "Dad was MIA from the start, and my mom worked her ass off till she died of a heart attack at forty-eight."

"I'm sorry." The words were so inadequate.

"Me, too. She was the hardest worker I ever met. She held down at least two and sometimes three jobs at a time. She made sure we never lost the house, and she made sure I had whatever I ridiculously thought I needed as a teenager. The newest jeans jacket, the stupid shoes. I thought I deserved those things because I was a latchkey kid from age five."

"My mom was always home, and then when she was gone, Bill was there. I always envied latchkey kids their freedom. We didn't even lock the door." He paused. "Still don't, now that I think about it."

"You don't lock your door?"

"It's Darling Bay."

She tugged at a silver chain around her neck, pulling it out of her shirt. "See this? My house key from then."

"Literally? The same key from when you were a kid?"

"The exact same one. I always wear it. Look, my mom had a word stamped on there in tiny letters."

He looked. Sure enough, in tiny all-caps, was the word *HOME*.

"She wanted to make sure I knew it wasn't just a house. That she worked so hard so we could have a home." Felicia's posture changed as her shoulders rolled forward. She dropped the key back into her shirt, and she got smaller. "It wasn't until I was an adult that I realized I might have been a latchkey kid *because* I wanted those expensive things— clothes and shoes and a bike and a computer—because my mom wanted to make me happy."

"That's not—" Liam wanted to reach for her, to unwrap her from the unhappy ball she'd become, but he had a feeling if he touched her, she'd snap.

"It's fine. I'm fine. That's where I got my love of television. She'd call me from whatever job she was at to make sure I was home. She didn't like me having people over, and she wasn't comfortable with me going to friends' houses, so I was alone. Just me and whatever sitcom or soap opera I was most into at the time. I fell in love with every hero on TV. Kind of the same way I fall in love with the stars on reality TV, too." She didn't feel stupid for saying it. He was listening to her. When was the last time someone had really done that, had listened so intently to her?

"So television is your family."

Felicia's mouth became a perfect O. "Oh, my god."

TWENTY-TWO

He was *right*. Holy crap. It wasn't just that she liked television because she'd watched so much of it as a kid. It was that television actually felt like *family*.

That was why she was loyal to it, why she was so loyal to her job. That's why she'd been able to forgo relationships and romantic vacations—she was involved with TV at work, and television shows at home. "That's the most succinct way of putting it I've ever heard. It kind of makes me feel…"

"Better, knowing that?"

"No. Like a complete loser, for never really seeing that before." At the moment, she had seventeen programs saved on her iPad. Those weren't for work, or for research. They were comfort viewing.

"You're not a loser."

Television was her addiction. Her drug. "Oh, my god, that is *sad*."

"Felicia—"

She shook her head. "I don't want to talk about it anymore." She would think about it later, when she was safely alone. She would figure out what to do with this new information. "If that's okay."

"Anything you want is okay."

That felt nice to hear. She smiled at him.

He didn't smile back. He just *looked* at her.

The air got thicker, warmer. Her chest heated.

"Thanks," Felicia managed.

Liam blinked, long and slow, keeping his eyes shut for half a second too long, opening them just as slowly. "You're welcome. But I can't remember for what. I lost track of the conversation."

Yeah, so did she. She wasn't thinking about the show, not anymore.

All she was thinking about was him kissing her again, like he had on her balcony.

Him kissing her hard.

And then, as if he could hear her wishing, he did.

He moved fast with a low growl that sent a shiver through her. Their mouths fit—she hadn't remembered that wrong. He kissed her hard and she kissed him back, and when his tongue stroked hers she couldn't keep from groaning. He tasted like hops and pineapple and she felt like she would never get enough of him. His mouth trailed down her neck, and she turned, impatient to have his lips against hers.

She twisted sideways, and then he was above her, his length pressed against hers. His knee went between hers, and she arched her hips upward, moving against his leg.

His eyes were darker blue now. "We should probably—"

"Mmm?" She could think of several things they should do. But she was *not* going to sleep with Liam on a rug that was a hundred years old.

But maybe on a sofa that was about the same age? That would be okay.

Liam pulled back and looked at her, as if trying to gauge exactly what she needed.

She wriggled sideways, out from under him, and then stood. He stood with her. He dropped his mouth to her neck again, pushing aside the errant strands, kissing his way up to her ear. "I want you," he said.

Her insides burst into flame. "Ditto." She turned so that his mouth was on hers again, and the kiss that followed engulfed her body in heat.

"We can take it slow, though." He stroked her jaw with his thumb.

"No."

"Sorry?" His voice had a catch in it.

"Not slow."

Liam pulled her against him, and she felt again how hard he was. "Are you sure?"

Funny, she was always unsure about sex. Usually she wondered if the timing was right, if she looked good enough, if she was with the right person.

Right now, though, she was dead sure about what she wanted.

And what she wanted was Liam. Inside her. Soon.

She reached her hands between them and undid his buckle.

Very soon.

"You haven't answered me." Liam stopped her hand gently.

She could feel him, hard and ready through his jeans, but his gaze was soft. "I'm sure."

"Sure sure?"

"I'm *so* fucking sure."

TWENTY-THREE

Liam laughed, and the sound of it was an aphro-disiac. She moved faster, and so did he. She shrugged out of his jacket, and then Liam tugged off her tank top. When his eyes narrowed with heat at the sight of her breasts, she was glad she'd been too lazy to put on a bra when she'd taken off her work clothes.

"You're incredible." His voice was low and rough.

This was when Liam would lean forward, and take her nipple into his mouth, and she couldn't wait for the heat and slickness of his lips—but he didn't.

He leaned forward, yes.

But then he tugged at the chain around her

neck. He lifted the key to his mouth, and kissed it gently, all the while keeping his soft gaze on hers.

And she melted inside. All her bones turned to liquid and her heart got too big to keep pounding in her chest, and she was suddenly too nervous to say another word, so she pulled hard at the fly of his jeans.

He laughed and the warm key fell back to her chest. She helped him out of his jeans, and then he returned the favor. Down to only their underwear, she straddled his lap as he sat on the edge of the sofa. He caught her mouth with his, and brought his hands to her cheeks. He decelerated, as surely as if a stop light had turned yellow.

The problem was that Felicia wanted a green light. And speed.

Liam drawled, "Slow down, sugar."

Felicia nipped at his bottom lip. "But I like fast."

She licked her way down his neck and then back up to his ear. Liam groaned. "Do you always get your way?"

"Only at work." But since work was her life... "Yes." She wrapped her legs around him tighter, and tilted her hips so that the only barrier between them was the cotton of his jockeys and the wet fabric of her panties.

"Well, hell. I *was* raised to be polite and give a

lady what she wants." He put his hands behind her neck and pulled her in tight. He kissed her hard, and left her no question about what would happen next.

Until he spoke.

"I'm going to ask, though, for a strange favor."

Felicia pulled back. "Should I be worried?"

"It might not feel natural."

She blinked. "Now I'm really nervous." She'd played some kinky games in the past, but was she ready to let a virtual stranger tie her up in a house in the middle of nowhere?

Well. It was Liam. She *might* let him do whatever the hell he wanted to her.

He laughed, a round, open sound. "You should be nervous. I want us both to face our fears, okay?"

Now she really *was* worried. "Um. What?"

He dropped his gaze, then appeared to take a breath. She could feel his chest expand beneath her hands. "Basically, I said on that stupid camera thing that I'm scared of people not accepting me if I show them who I am. And you said you're scared to feel your feelings. So I'm going to suggest that if we shimmy all the way down to naked, and I really hope we do," he moved against her as if to prove it, "then let's both of us do what we're scared to do."

If he'd suggested tying her upside down and

whipping her with Red Vines, she would have been less surprised. She was staggered. *"Oh."*

He put his hand against her heart, and she felt her nipple tighten just below his fingers. "You feel. I'll show you who I am. Neither of us will be scared."

"I can try." She wanted to. Felicia really wanted to.

He leaned back into the sofa, taking her with him. Then he rolled, so that he was on top of her, holding his weight on his elbows. "Naked shimmy now?"

Felicia kissed him as she wriggled out of her panties, and kept kissing him while she tugged down his shorts. Condom, oh, condom, damn her, what had she been thinking? She should've already handled this —

Liam kissed her right breast, taking the nipple into his mouth and sucking gently. "Gorgeous," he said around it. "You're fucking gorgeous."

Condom, condom. Felicia flailed her arm toward her purse, which was six feet away, at least.

"Want to see a magic trick?"

She was finally able to get the breath to say the word. "Condom!"

Liam snapped next to her ear. Then he brought his hand in front of her face, flipping a wrapped condom from finger to finger.

"I'm going to need you to explain how you did that." Felicia ripped the wrapper off. "Later. Right now, I need you to do something else."

His shaft was so hot she wondered if the condom would melt. Or if she would. It didn't seem out of the realm of possibility. She reached down between them and rolled the latex over his cock. He was still propped up on his elbows, and she could feel the tension in his muscles. One of them was shaking, but she wasn't sure which of them it was.

Liam kissed her again. "We can go as slow as we—"

Him and his polite yellow stop light. She wanted it to go green. "Fast."

His eyes lit with heat, and he thrust into her fully, hard and fast.

She gasped as it felt like all the air was pushed out of her lungs. He was big—just enough to stretch her, just enough to hit the very back of what she could take.

He was just fucking right.

And he was still on his elbows, as if he wanted to keep his weight off her, to keep her safe.

That was the thing, though. She felt safe.

And more than that, she *felt*. So much.

So she told him. "You're perfect. You are totally, completely perfect."

He gave a low moan in her ear and started to

move. She lifted her hips to meet him, to match him with every stroke. He pulled his head back to watch her, and she'd never felt more beautiful. The harder and hotter he got and the faster he moved, the darker his eyes became.

Felicia had never been a talker in bed before. But every word she said to him made her get wetter, and every word seemed to turn him on more. "Liam, oh, god. You fit me. You *fit* me. Jesus, Liam, please don't stop. Please—don't—stop." Each word did something to her, to him— she didn't think it was because the words were dirty. He was *listening*. As if he was hearing more than her words, more than she could say out loud. As if he could *hear* her feelings, even if she didn't know what they were. "Please don't stop, *please don't stop.*"

She meant it—she wanted this to go on forever. Could it, please? How could she make that happen? She'd do anything to keep it going, but she was getting closer to orgasm with every move. Every thrust brought her clit into contact with his pubic bone, and every stroke lifted her breath into the top of her lungs, as all parts south of her navel contracted into one fine, perfect, trembling tight point. She wasn't going to be able to help it—she couldn't stop—

Felicia lost the ability to speak, to come up with even one more word, and then he spoke low in her ear. "I hear you. I hear you."

She came so hard it felt like an explosion, shrapnel taking off the top of her head. Lights flashed behind her eyelids. She shattered.

And she'd never be able to put herself back together again. *He heard her.*

Then he came with a roar, and she wrapped herself around him, holding him, catching him.

He collapsed on top of her, a sweet, heavy weight that felt like safety, like contentment.

"Felicia. Sweet Jesus." He lifted his head to look at her.

She turned her face—he'd see the tears that had suddenly sprung to her eyes but—

"I heard you," he said.

You're everything. She couldn't say it.

Not now, not when she could barely breathe for happiness and the fear that filled in behind it.

TWENTY-FOUR

Liam woke, confused at first. He was happy—so stupid-happy—but why? And where was he?

The room smelled like dust and fresh wood. And sex.

Felicia.

She was the reason his arm had fallen asleep. They were still on the sofa. Sometime in the middle of the night, he'd gotten up and explored closets until he'd found an old wool blanket. It was scratchy, but Felicia's skin was so soft she made up for the itch. Her head rested on his bicep, and she gave a soft little "pah" every time she exhaled. He'd never heard a cuter noise in his life.

He reached as carefully as he could for his cell phone. Her breathing didn't even change.

Good, it was still early. He could stay like this with her for another thirty minutes before going to pick up Timbo from the school sleep-over. Automatically, he opened his email to see if there were any fires that needed putting out.

Nothing was in flames, but there were two emails from Felicia about filming with his brothers, and one reply from Aidan.

She'd been working. While he'd been sleeping. He'd been on the sofa naked with her, and she'd been sending work email.

Carefully, he pulled his arm out from under her head. He rubbed his face and his eyes. What did her working while he slept mean? Had he missed something? A cue of some sort? Was he so boring that she just waited for him to sleep before going back to work?

As he stared at the screen, a text landed from Timbo. *I can't wait for today. I'm going to be the best intern they ever had.*

He had thought he'd have at least a couple more days before they started shooting in earnest. Maybe a little more time to spend with Felicia. He really knew nothing about television production, that much was obvious. This pace was so fast, so immediate. Felicia needed to spend some more time in this town, and maybe she'd learn what it felt like to slow down, to watch a sunset, to lie in bed and drowsily think about how good the coffee would taste.

"Oh, my god, what time is it?" Felicia sat straight up as if a string had yanked her out from under the blanket.

"Not even eight yet. We have time. Good morning, gorgeous—" *Gorgeous?* Lame. That was probably what every man called her. He wanted to find a name to call her that suited her—that suited the way he was feeling.

Good morning, love.

No.

He was crazy. It had just been sex.

But it had been sex with a woman he wanted to spend a really long, slow time getting to know better. She'd spoken her feelings to him, even though she'd said she wasn't good at it. He'd told her his fear, that opening up to someone would lead to pain.

And she'd kissed him in response.

He wanted to spend the day with her, *not* working. He wanted to spend the week with her. The year.

More.

He was nuts.

Gorgeous would have to do.

But she wasn't listening anyway. She was up and off the sofa without even a morning kiss. Was this the way she always got up? As if she woke with an engine already going full throttle?

Lucky for him, she was still stark naked and didn't seem to mind that he was staring. All that soft brown skin, those incredible breasts that he'd teased and tasted last night...

Felicia didn't even seem to notice his staring as she pulled on her clothes. "Holy crap, I've got to get back, get a shower, change my clothes, and then be back here in less than two hours."

He folded his hands behind his head and leaned against the padded arm of the sofa. "Are we really in such a hellfire hurry?"

"You might not be." She reached under the low table for a shoe. "But this is my job."

"So you like it?" Liam yawned and stretched his arms up and overhead. "The job, I mean."

She glanced at him. Even in her fevered state, without a lick of makeup and with a serious case of bed head, Felicia was amazing. Electricity seemed to spark from her miles of exposed skin, and he wanted to feel that current again, to feel every inch of her.

"It's all I ever wanted."

"So it's your dream job."

"Yep."

"What happens when someone like you reaches all your goals?"

She seemed to stumble for a second. "I guess—I guess you're happy."

Last night, she had seemed to be. He didn't take the credit for that, as much as he would like to. She'd not only made love openly and joyfully, she'd seemed to really be *with* him the whole time. Her face had been happy when he kissed her the last time, right before he fell asleep.

Was she running away now? Or just honestly in a hurry?

"I have to pee." She padded out of the room.

Liam pulled on his jeans and shirt. Her necklace with the key on it had fallen to the floor—he tucked it into his pocket to make sure it stayed safe.

He looked at his phone for a few minutes.

A response email came from Felicia to Aidan.

She was literally in the bathroom, working.

This was ridiculous.

He went to the bathroom door. He listened, but heard nothing but the *bing* that sounded like an email landing.

Liam knocked.

The door cracked open. She wore a smile, but he couldn't read it. Was she annoyed? Or amused?

"It's been so long," she said.

"I had an idea for our date. But I'm going to keep it a secret until we go on it. Will you trust me?"

He watched her blink. He watched her think about the question. Damn if it should be this hard to decide.

"Remember it has to be filmed."

"That's not an answer."

"Yes." She licked her bottom lip and opened the door wider. "I trust you. Don't you have to go pick up Timbo or something?"

"Yeah, in about half an hour. Tell me something. Did you really get up and send work emails in the middle of the night?"

"Sometimes work helps me sleep." She slipped past him and back into the parlor, where she searched her purse for something.

He trailed behind her. "Sometimes having amazing sex helps *me* sleep. It doesn't work that way for you?" Stuck overnight on a couch with a long, leggy, naked brunette like Felicia, he'd have been in no hurry to do a title search or pull a credit report, no matter how eager the client was. "Hey. Know what?"

"What?" She looked up him and then back into her purse. Her lashes were thick and clumped. He remembered them dropping lazily to her cheeks after her third orgasm the night before. She put a piece of gum in her mouth and held out the pack toward him. "Not as good as a toothbrush but it's all I've got."

He took a piece. "You don't have to be scared, you know."

She chewed faster. "I'm not."

"Okay. I am, though."

"Why? Of what? What are you talking about?" Her words tumbled out quickly. Too quickly. She *was* frightened of this—whatever this was between them.

"I like you a lot. A *lot* a lot. I want to get to know you better. I know I'm acting like a damn golden retriever or something, but I get excited about things. That's just me. I'm glad we're doing this, and I'm glad you're going to let me show you Darling Bay."

"Look. I never stop working, Liam." She snapped her purse closed. "That was fun last night. Don't get me wrong. Working is just who I am. I'm boring. Don't worry, though." Felicia tugged on her second heel. "We can find a way to get you the bonus, even with the physical contact clause out of the contract. If that's what you're worried about."

Liam felt his jaw literally drop. "Jesus." Sex *meant* something to him. And that's why he belonged in Northern California. "I'm just going to pretend you didn't insult me like that."

"No, I thought—"

He reached for his socks, and then his boots. He

sat on the most uncomfortable chair in the world and tried to suck up his disappointment.

She was from LA, he had to remember that. The pace there was a thousand times faster. Did sex not mean as much there? "You thought that's why we hooked up?" Such a casual way to reference what they'd done to each other in the middle of the night. Over and over.

"No."

He narrowed his eyes, and she relented.

"Okay," she said. "I wasn't sure."

"You *should* be sure about how I felt last night." How he felt now, in the light of day was something he couldn't even guess at.

Felicia shook her head. "I don't—"

"It's okay. It's totally fine." He pulled on his second boot and pushed a big old fake smile onto his face. His jaw was so stiff it hurt. "It's all good. I'll see you back here later, okay?"

"Liam. Don't just go."

But how could he stay?

As he got into his car, he didn't let himself glance in the rearview mirror at himself. He was pretty sure he looked just the same, even though he felt completely different. Liam was confident he was a good guy. But a woman like Felicia didn't fall for a simple, good guy. Someone in her line of work would inevitably fall for a wealthy plastic surgeon who ran marathons and ate Paleo.

He didn't even jog.

He was just a guy who sold houses while trying to be a good foster dad.

A foster dad who was going to be late picking up his son if he didn't hit the gas.

So he did. And if his wheels spun out as he went, maybe that was just eagerness to get away.

TWENTY-FIVE

Showered and changed, Felicia drove back to the treehouse.

She'd felt like an asshole plenty of times. Living in LA got a person used to that. You were never going to merge into the next lane if you didn't feel comfortable with your hand on the horn.

But damn it, she felt like a jerk.

Liam had labeled himself a golden retriever, but that wasn't quite right. She thought of golden retrievers as eager but dumb, and Liam was smart as hell. The night before, he'd matched everything she'd thrown at him, both verbally and physically.

She'd fit in his arms. He'd felt so right. He'd lowered her mouth to the most intimate places on her body, but first he'd kissed her *key*.

And that fact made her as nervous as a nineteen-year-old PA on her first day on set.

She shouldn't have sent the email to Natasha. It had been automatic. She hadn't felt badly about sending it till it whooshed away from her phone.

She'd sat on the toilet seat in the middle of the night, her legs still aching, and she'd panicked. She'd held out her hands and watched them tremble.

With cold? With tension?

No, she'd been shaking with feelings that she didn't *want* to flood her body. Feelings sucked. This proved it.

She typed it out on her phone. *He's scared of losing everyone. Neither of his parents wanted him, his foster father died, his fiancé left him.*

She couldn't tell Natasha this. It would be the betrayal he was scared of.

Yeah, and these feelings—the ones that told her to stand, to leap back onto the sofa and into his arms, the ones that said to wrap her arms around Liam for the next hundred years or so—that's what *she* was most scared of.

They were both doing this for money. She needed to remember that. This was business.

This was her job.

So sitting in the bathroom in the middle of the night, Felicia had hit send.

If she'd been trying to be fair, she would have told Natasha what *she'd* said, too. But confessing to her boss that TV was not only Felicia's job but also a substitute for Felicia's family and her feelings?

She hadn't been able to admit that to Natasha.

But Felicia would fix it. She'd lure Natasha with something bigger. Better. Maybe she'd admit to her boss that she and Liam *had* hooked up off camera. Then Natasha would work so hard to get them to repeat the night on-camera (tasteful night-vision camera, a closed door at the last moment) that she'd forget the email. Worst case scenario, Felicia would tell Liam what she'd told Natasha—tell him that Natasha couldn't make use of any part of it without him agreeing to it. She would explain.

The rental lurched over a pothole in the driveway that was getting bigger by the day. She parked under the biggest oak tree, near the canteen truck.

The set—because that's what it was, after all, it wouldn't be her house until she spent a night in her bed with no cameras around—was a mad scramble already. There were two new trucks loaded with heavy equipment that hadn't been there the day before. Four guys were unloading supplies onto a dolly. The canteen had already been set up to the right of the house. Everything looked so festive that the house could have been the site of a wedding about to take place, some happy celebration that would bring friends and family back to town.

Instead, it was a television show. A program that would matter to the people who watched it until they flipped off the television and went to bed. *She* was the one this mattered to the most. As a producer, she was used to that feeling, but it was multiplied by ten now. This would be her home. For whatever reason, this was where she wanted to spread her roots into the soil.

If she let herself feel it, she would be terrified.

So naturally, she cut the feeling right off like she was silencing her phone. She could almost feel the switch flipping in her mind.

Work. She was at *work*.

A man strode toward her. He was tall and rangy, with bright blue eyes. He wore a gray T-shirt that might have once been black, and a tool belt dropped low on his hips. Timbo walked next to him.

She stepped forward and shook his hand. "I'm Felicia Turbinado, and you're Aidan Ballard. Nice to see you in person, and not on Skype."

"Good to meet you. My brother said to tell you he'll be a little late, but I brought Timbo here with me."

Felicia stuck out her hand, but the boy surprised her, going in for a hug. He smelled like soap and something salty, maybe potato chips?

"I can't *wait*. I couldn't even sleep last night at the overnighter. I told all the guys, and they're super jealous, and I was just wondering if maybe I would be onscreen at all? Because I don't even think they *believe* what I'm doing today. But if they saw me on TV, maybe then they would."

"Well, I can tell you this. I'm going to assign you to work with Anna. She runs a camera, and if she thinks it's a good idea that you're on screen, then it might happen. But that's only if you do everything she says."

"Where is she?"

Felicia pointed to where Anna was setting up a door shot. "Go introduce yourself."

He was off like a shot, Aidan smiling after him. "He's a good kid. I'm glad you're giving him a chance. Every kid deserves one, and him more than most."

A chance.

Maybe she should give Liam one, too.

Nervousness flapped in her chest. "Okay, then! Hopefully you're better in front of the camera than your brother was, and hopefully I'm a little more relaxed today, too. We have a *lot* of work to do."

The next three hours flew by, as they shot and reshot interior scenes. Aidan proved a natural, his thumbs tucked into his toolbelt as he jaw-jacked with the crew, ready with a quick and friendly laugh. Felicia couldn't know for sure until she met Jake in person, but she had a feeling Aidan would be the biggest draw of the show.

That made it all the better that she was going on the date with Liam and not Aidan. Women would fall for the construction guy and tune into the next episode that much more eagerly.

Excellent. All for the network.

While they reshot a room walk-through, Felicia found herself reaching for the key around her neck. It wasn't there—she must have left it at the Cat's Meow.

Pull it together.

This was work.

Luckily, Felicia and Aidan agreed on almost everything. He thought the rusted-through clawfoot tub had to go, but he knew about a new kind of spa tub that would fit in the same place and still look vintage. Upstairs, he was going to make half the great room into the bedroom of her dreams, and split the rest of the space into two offices. Each room's focus would be the redwood, and the way it grew up and out.

Aidan looked up at the canvas-covered space between the tree and the great outdoors. "That's been keeping out leaks just fine, but I'm thinking we can widen the hole in the ceiling and make it into a skylight, so you'll get a better visual upward."

"Yeah!" Timbo's voice trumpeted through the great room. "So you can see right up to the top tree-house!" Production had loaned Timbo a spare handheld camera, just for fun and the outside chance of possible extra footage, and he was eagerly zooming in and out on everything that caught his eye.

Felicia nodded. "I love that idea. In the bedroom, you mean?"

"We can carry the skylight through into both offices, too." Aidan didn't even glance at the camera Tony had trained on him. He was going to be great.

"But I only need one office, don't I?"

Aidan tapped on a wall with a heavy hand. He listened for something she couldn't hear. "One full office. One secondary office with just a small desk, and a spare bed for guests. That'll be for the nursery, too."

Felicia dropped the measuring tape she'd been holding for him, and it clattered on the wood floor. "The what?"

Both Tony's and Timbo's cameras panned to focus on Felicia's face.

"The nursery. You eventually want a kid or two, right?"

"That's nothing I'm thinking of right now."

"It's my job to think of the eventualities, your job to tell me what style you want."

Felicia took two quick, deep breaths. "Exactly what we saw downstairs. Old-fashioned, turn-of-the-century, and quaint."

"Quaint but modern," Aidan corrected her.

"That."

"Just one baby, then."

Felicia squeaked loudly. Embarrassingly. *Always professional.*

Everyone laughed.

So she pretended her phone was vibrating with a call, and she raced from the room, her steps as fast as her racing heart.

———

AS THEY WRAPPED the set for the day, Felicia got better at juggling her producer and client hats. She made sure they got a clip of her asking how long the work would take.

Aidan said, "A couple of weeks. Maybe three."

Felicia feigned surprise. "That fast?"

He leaned against a door jam. "We're a full-service crew and I hired extra guys to work fast. This'll be easy. We're only pulling out the one wall, and all your electricity and plumbing is in pretty good shape for a house this old. We'll paint and refinish the floors. The bathroom will take the longest, but barring dry rot, we'll be good. Now I guess all you have to do is pick a brother."

Felicia hadn't even written that line for him. He really *was* a natural. She felt stilted and awkward next to him. "For the date? I guess...I'll choose Liam."

"What about Jake? You haven't even met him yet, have you?"

Felicia shook her head. She felt her cheeks color. Aidan was driving this, not her. But that was okay, the Ballard Brothers were the draw, after all. "Jake's the sailor, right? I don't like boats much."

Aidan gave a nod. "Yep. Then you are *all* the way out of his running, I'm sorry to tell you. He'll be here on the crew tomorrow, and I'll make sure I tell him not to invite you to his Fourth of July party on the water. And what, I'm just out of the running, too?"

"Sorry, but I..." *I spent the night in your brother's arms, and I might never recover.* "I like a man good with numbers."

And good with his hands.

And his mouth.

And his words.

Oh, lord. She was in so much trouble.

TWENTY-SIX

Liam spent the day in the office, licking his wounds. Okay, just one wound. But it was a big one, and it hurt.

It was fine—he had plenty of work to do. The show was generating crazy amounts of paperwork. He probably didn't need to go over every single line-item the way he was, but it was giving him something to do. He had to make sure they sneaked in no more sex clauses, after all.

Had Felicia really thought that? That he'd slept with her for a potential bonus?

Yeah. That was some bullshit.

Liam took a break at one and delivered a crapload of sandwiches to the boys playing hoops at the school.

"Where's Timbo?"

"No, really? Tell us the truth!"

"He said he's gonna be on TV!"

"He said he's gonna be famous!"

Liam tossed sandwiches at the boys as if they were starving lions. Four bites each, and every sandwich was gone. "He might be on TV, probably won't be famous, at least not yet."

"Are *you* gonna be famous?"

Liam shook his head.

"He's lying. Timbo said it was going to be the biggest new show ever."

"Guys! It's not a big deal."

He didn't even believe it himself.

Liam left the extra sandwiches (only two, both bologna and mustard) for later, and went back to the office for a few more hours.

At four, he drove to the treehouse to pick up Timbo. Liam's chest was tight as he pulled up the driveway.

He didn't want to see Felicia.

And he wanted nothing else in his whole damn life.

Today the house really looked like a movie set. It was mobbed, full of people he'd never seen before running in all directions. Aidan had handled today's shooting with Felicia—it was all about the remodel, and Liam hadn't been needed. Honestly, he hadn't felt like being there.

Now he wondered if he should have been.

Aidan was a little bit taller than Liam or Jake. He had the brightest blue eyes of all of them. He swaggered just that much more.

Liam had never been jealous of Aidan in his life, had never begrudged him one single female conquest.

But god help him if his brother tried to muscle in on Felicia.

Timbo came out the small front door. His face lit up when he saw Liam. "Hey! They totally let me hold the camera."

"Yeah? You ready to go?"

As Timbo walked next to Liam on the way to the car, he practically levitated. "Did you hear me? They let me film some stuff!"

"I heard you. That's cool."

"It *was*. You don't know what footage—that's what they call it—they're gonna use until they're editing it, and that doesn't happen here, well, I mean they have a little editing studio, but that's not where they do the big work. That's in LA. And Anna said that if I go see her the next time I'm in town, she'll give me a tour of the studio, and she said that I'll see at least a couple of movie stars, if not more." He bounced his way to the car.

His phone pinged with a text. *I'm sorry about saying that about the bonus. I hurt your feelings. I didn't mean to. Sometimes I forget the Hollywood way isn't normal. Again, sorry.*

A rubber band of tightness eased in his chest. Liam looked over his shoulder at the house. "Did you see Felicia today? Is she still here?"

"Duh. She and Uncle Aidan made all sorts of decisions about where to put things like beds and shit."

"Language." He didn't really care, though. All boys swore. "Did they get along?"

They got in the car, and Liam let Timbo fiddle with the stereo until he couldn't stand it anymore. "Did you hear me?"

"What?"

"Did Felicia and Uncle Aidan get along? Is she still here somewhere?"

"They got along just fine, I think, but like I said, I was running the camera, so I was pretty busy. He made her laugh a lot."

"He did?" The stereo blared, and his head started hurting.

"Yeah, I think they were going to go and get something to eat."

"Oh." Liam started the car and then backed it carefully around a UPS van that had just raced up the driveway.

"Oh, my god, you should *see* your face right now." Timbo bent forward with laughter.

"Excuse me?"

"Uncle Aidan gave me five bucks to say that to you. He told me it would be worth it even if you got mad. And he was right! They didn't go out to eat. Felicia said she had work to do tonight, but she said she was looking forward to seeing you tomorrow for your date." Timbo made his voice girlish on the last two words, and Liam could practically see the SnapChat hearts floating above the word *date*.

"You suck."

"Language!"

"Suck isn't a bad word."

Timbo shot him a surprisingly wry look with one eyebrow lifted. "I was *referring* to the word you didn't say between *you* and *suck*."

"What do I always tell you?"

"You can't get in trouble if you don't say it."

"That's it." Felicia was looking forward to the date. Liam's heart was suddenly so light it was a good thing he didn't drive a convertible. He held out his hand for a high five, and Timbo slapped it so hard he knew he'd feel the tingle for the next five minutes.

And when Timbo turned the music up to eleven, Liam didn't turn it down. Let the kid be happy. It felt good.

TWENTY-SEVEN

The next day, Natasha called while Felicia was finishing getting ready for The Date. She'd put it capitals in her mind, and they'd stayed there.

The Date.

On camera.

"So what are you two doing?" Natasha's voice was quick, clipped. She was calling to make sure whatever they did would look good on film, no matter what. She'd been horrified to find out they were going to stay in Darling Bay. "Bowling? I'm picturing you in a yellowed button-down shirt that says *Buster* on the pocket."

Felicia sighed. Oh, man, this was going to suck. Liam hadn't even found her on set when he'd picked up Timbo the day before, and he'd stayed away all day today, too. He was probably still furious. The Date had been set up on email. *I'll pick you in front of The Cat's Meow at six.*

The email had felt perfunctory. Romance didn't enter into it.

Felicia tried to smooth her hair with one hand while holding the phone with her other. "I don't know. He's making it a surprise."

"Well, don't blow it."

"Thanks for the vote of confidence."

"Oh, come on. It's not like this is a normal date for you. And I take it back, you're allowed to blow it only if you do it spectacularly. Do you think you can cry on cue?"

"Oh, my god." Felicia rummaged in her bag for her necklace, but she must have dropped it at the house after she'd slept with Liam. She'd find it later, though she wanted it *now*. "It's not like this would be a normal date for anyone, including you. If this show flies, this particular date will be witnessed by millions." Her stomach churned at the thought, and she was glad she'd only had a light lunch.

"Don't be nervous, and of course the show will fly. You forget who I am. Now, you should laugh, but not too much. And don't forget to mention his brothers, since they'll be the reason people tune back in."

For a brief moment, Felicia felt like crying. This

already meant too much, and it was nothing but a forty-eight minute segment of a series she'd have to continue to produce. With Liam and his brothers. The pressure was too great. If only she hadn't sent the pictures of the treehouse to Natasha, if only Natasha hadn't picked it as the one. Then Felicia would have been able to buy the house quietly with no fanfare, and none of the rest of this would be happening.

Of course, that meant Liam would go on a date with someone else. A different woman, looking at a different house.

Gah. The way her stomach dropped at the thought made Felicia question what the hell she was doing. What she wanted.

Her job. She wanted her great job. And the amazing house.

Liam.

No, no, *no*, not romance, not love. She'd always been fine without the real thing. She had the other real (fake) thing, right in front of her, all the time. And that had to be okay. Felicia was there first to do her job, and only second to buy a home she hadn't known could be real.

She was *not* there to fall in love with anything but her new house. Felicia wasn't the mark. She was the producer, the one who made the plan, the one who called the shots.

Natasha was still giving her instructions. "Don't dress up too much, and don't wear red, you'll wash out on camera. But don't underdress. Wait, just tell me what you're wearing."

Natasha was the boss. Felicia did what she said. Those were the rules, that was how the game was played.

Felicia looked down at the red dress she'd put on, at her red heels. She looked good in red, and at this very moment, she didn't care what she she'd look like on camera.

She cared how she looked in front of Liam. That was all. Screw the camera.

"Felicia? Are you there?"

"I can't—you—what are you—so much static—call you back!" Felicia's heart raced. Hanging up on Natasha could be a terminable offense.

Felicia had never done a thing to threaten her dream job. She was a model employee, happily neglecting her real life for the sake of the network.

What if what she wanted in her real life was changing?

The thought made her chest feel icy inside.

She switched her phone to silent, and then she went outside to stand in the afternoon sun. Liam would be there any minute.

As she leaned against the red gate and tried to ignore that Pearl Hawthorne was peering out the breakfast room's window at her, Felicia tried to sort out what she was feeling.

She was so bad at it. Was nervousness a feeling? Or was that just something her body was doing? Should she feel dread? Was worry a feeling or a thing to do?

The rusty old truck that she'd seen parked in front of Liam's home-office turned the corner. It slowed in front of her, bumping its wheel on the curb. The passenger-side window cranked down. "Looking for a ride, little lady?" The grin that spread across Liam's jaw was enormous, and it told her that he'd forgiven her for thinking (only for a second!) that he'd slept with her for a possible payout.

She didn't even care that there was a camera on the dashboard, and that Tony and Gene were trailing behind the truck in a rented Toyota hybrid.

Suddenly, Felicia knew what she felt.

She felt excited. And she felt happy.

And she didn't want to stop feeling either way.

TWENTY-EIGHT

Felicia looked surprised when he pulled up, and Liam didn't blame her. This wasn't his work car. There was no leather inside, and it smelled more like diesel fumes than air freshener. It was Bill's old truck, the one the brothers shared between them. Sometimes it was Aidan's work truck, and sometimes Jake used it for delivery if he pulled a lot of crab. Tonight, it was the date-mobile, and Liam was pretty sure it had never had a more important task.

She also looked incredible. Hot red dress, high red fuck-me heels. Her lipstick matched, and he wanted to kiss it off as soon as was humanly possible.

Instead, though, he just got out and opened the passenger door for her. Lord, he'd forgotten how much the metal screeched on this old rust bucket. The camera crew, because of course there was one, filmed him helping Felicia in. They were probably highly amused by the choice of transportation, but he didn't care. This was the truck he loved, and he wanted to show Felicia the important things.

Felicia settled herself in without complaint, her eyes bright.

Liam felt more hope than should have been legal to possess. He felt high with it.

He'd planned every minute of their afternoon and evening, and this date was going to be perfect.

They went to the Golden Spike café first, for a quick quesadilla and one of Molly Darling's famous chocolate malts. Molly and Nikki played off each other well in front of the cameras, exchanging light-hearted banter over the heads of the regulars and tourists alike. The sheriff, who happened to be Molly's boyfriend, stopped by to say hi and raise hell with a group of skateboarders in front of the restaurant. There was shouting, and then the sheriff was *on* a skateboard, trying a trick, and it all smoothed out. The cook somehow managed to catch a pan of fish fritters on fire in the kitchen, and the arrival of the fire department just made everything more exciting.

Their next stop was the beach. They walked to the end of the pier, and he showed her how to throw corn chips up into the air so that the seagulls caught them in their beaks while diving. The camera crew (which thankfully didn't include Timbo, who was staying overnight on Jake's boat) thought this was fun, and got into the action. Tony and Gene went through more than half of Liam's bag of corn chips.

This wasn't so much as a date as it was a team-building exercise, apparently.

"So, yeah. This is one of the things we do for fun around here." Liam said it to the camera, but Felicia was the one who smiled at him.

"I love it. Just a sec." Felicia flagged down Anna, who had been making notes on a clipboard. "Hey, make sure you get some good shots of the surfers, okay?"

Anna nodded, and the crew headed to mid-pier, where the view of the surfers playing dodge with the tar-stained pilings was best.

For a moment, they were alone.

In a move that surprised him, Felicia slid her hand into his. "I'm sorry this is such a freak show."

"I'm not sure if I would call it that, but it's definitely not the..."

Felicia looked up at him, her eyes soft. "Go on."

"It's not the date I would take you on, if I had a choice."

"But—"

"I mean, it's the date I planned. If it was just me and you, I'd be better at talking."

"You're doing just fine."

"As soon as those cameras are focused on me, I forget every smart thing I was planning to say. And the fact that you look incredible isn't helping me any." Liam didn't even mean it as a compliment. It was just a statement of fact. The red dress had a low cut vee and tank top straps. It nipped in at her waist, then it flared out until it ended right at the top of her calves. Behind that particular calf was a soft velvety place his lips had enjoyed tracing just two nights before. Felicia's long hair was softly waved and hung loose around her face. The ocean breeze played with the strands the way he wanted to. Her lips were dark red and glossed, as if she'd just licked them, another thing he wanted to do again.

He could wrap his arm around her—he could kiss her right here—

And then Anna and her crew were back. The boom mic dangled over their heads like an ominous black seagull. Whenever Felicia and Liam spoke to each other, the crew kept their eyes averted, as if doing so would make them feel more at ease, to give them more privacy.

But it wasn't working.

"I'm sorry. This isn't ideal." Felicia tucked a

strand of hair behind her ear. "But it's you. And me. And I'm glad of that."

He leaned over the railing. "You know what else we do in this town for fun?" He directed the sentence directly at Felicia, determined to ignore the fact that not just six pairs of eyes were trained on him, but that millions eventually would be.

Felicia's hand was still in his, small and warm. "What?"

"We jump."

"Seriously?" Felicia leaned over the railing, too. "But we're so high up, and what about the pilings?"

"We're not that high, and you just have to make sure you jump outward."

"Has anyone ever died doing it?"

"There are a couple of legends that say a kid did once, but nobody knows if that's true or not."

Felicia looked thrilled. "Have *you* done it?"

Liam tried to sound casual. "Of course."

"How many times?"

"Okay. I only did it once on grad night. I was drunk, and stupid, and I was just lucky I swam in the right direction."

She squeezed his hand. "I can just see you. Young and stupid."

"The only thing different is that I'm not that young anymore." He turned so that he was facing Felicia.

Felicia watched him carefully, steadily, as if the commotion of the crew around her didn't bother her. "It's beautiful here."

"It looks even better from the water. Want to jump?"

"*What?*"

"Right now." Liam could actually hear the camera's lens zooming in.

She looked down at her clothes. "This is a brand-new dress. Dry-clean only, I think."

"What is it that you like about reality TV?"

Felicia met his gaze, and she appeared to take the question seriously. "I like the reality part. The fact that usually it's about a fantasy life that comes true, in part. Maybe it doesn't come together in the way that the participant hopes for, but it's actually their real *lives* on camera."

"So it's not real but it's real. Okay. And what qualities does a good reality TV star have?"

Felicia touched the place at her neck where her key usually hung. "Hope. They always have a lot of hope, even if they don't know they do. They're bold. They're brave. Even when they're acting a certain way because they're scared, the fact that they're on screen means that they're brave, deep down inside, no matter what anyone says about them."

"So you're brave. You're bold."

"You're trying to trick me into jumping into the ocean."

"No tricks up these sleeves. Of course," he unbuttoned the top button of his shirt. "I'll have to take off my shirt to prove that to you."

"*Naked* jumping?"

She shook her head, but there was a light behind her eyes.

Liam undid the next button. "I'm getting naked because I intend to continue this date, and I want to do it in dry clothes." They'd blur out the naughty bits, and if America noticed that he was carrying fifteen more pounds than he had in college, he didn't give a good rat's ass.

"Liam—"

"Guess where the cameras won't be able to follow us?" Liam shot what he hoped was a cheeky wink at the camera closest to him.

"Good *point*." Felicia closed her eyes, as if doing the math in her head that would allow to her to move. "Good point," she repeated, seemingly more to herself than him.

She was fast—faster than he was. One quick *zip* and she was standing on the pier in her bra, panties and heels. Liam struggled with the last button, and then Felicia stepped close enough to him to help him with his belt.

Just like she had on the sofa in the treehouse.

Luckily, the thought of being seen by millions of people prevented him from popping wood, but just barely. He got out of his shoes and his pants, and then shucked off his shorts.

She was naked then, her clothes in a small pile. Her nipples were bright pink and tightly budded, and her long legs just accentuated the gorgeous swell of her hips. She turned to face Gene and Tony and said, "You laugh at me and you're fired."

Their cameras kept filming, but the men stared at the ground, their faces red. Anna just looked shocked.

Felicia was glorious. She was a Venus, and Liam should be finding her a scallop shell to step out of—she was that radiant.

He could look at her all day.

"All right, you." Felicia stepped up the first rung of the railing. "Coming with me? Hey, Anna, get Production to have our clothes and two towels each waiting for us on the shore."

Anna barked an order one direction, and then another one at Tony. "Get under the pier. *Hurry*. At least get footage of the swim in!"

TWENTY-NINE

What was she *doing?* Felicia was butt-ass naked on national television, and even worse than that, she was naked in front of her *staff,* in front of the crew she'd hired.

The water below seemed a long way down. It couldn't have been more than twenty feet, but that was eighteen feet too many. "I don't..."

Liam joined her on the railing. "What's that, sugar?"

He looked hot as hell. Not many people could carry this off. She'd worked with some contestants that they might have paid just to keep their clothes *on.* Not this guy. Liam was long and rangy, with that subtle six-pack at his abs and that softness in those eyes that were as light blue as the cloudless sky behind him. He could stand up here with her all day long. She wouldn't mind the fact that she was naked as long as she could keep looking at him. "I was just going to say that...I'm scared." Jesus, it was another feeling. What was Liam doing to her?

"Then take my hand."

She could still back out. She could step off the railing and slink back into her clothes.

But then she'd have to come up with a reason why she didn't jump, a reason that was better than simple fear.

And wasn't this kind of bravery exactly why she liked to watch reality TV from the safety of her own couch, popcorn bowl in her lap? Low stakes, maybe, but still, this would require a chutzpah she'd never had.

Felicia was boring. She worked hard, and she played things safe.

She was scared.

How often was she scared and didn't even notice?

She didn't want to be the same Felicia she'd always been. At least not with Liam. She wanted to be more than that, even for just a fraction of a moment. She took a breath and held it. Then she said, "Okay."

They both turned to face the water. Liam took her hand.

"Don't let go." She squeezed his hand as hard as she could.

"Okay."

Felicia felt the eyes of her crew on her ass. Suddenly not giving one good goddamn what anyone thought of her at all, she shook her bottom. She heard Anna give a muffled laugh. "When do we jump?" The fear was in her again, climbing.

Liam dropped his mouth to hers in a quick kiss.

That was for the cameras, she could feel it. It was a polite kiss. His lips stayed closed. Then against her mouth, he said, "*Now*."

The word, his word, gave her the bravery to go. Together, they jumped.

The fall took forever—it took an eternity to hit the surface and her stomach did somersaults the whole way down—but Liam held her hand tightly the whole time, not breaking contact until they were under the cold water, swimming their way up to the light. They came up gasping, laughing. She felt frozen—stiff and oxygen-less—and so *alive* at the same time.

"Cold! So cold!" Felicia sputtered and spit out of a mouthful of salt water. "Jesus jumping Christ, is this water made from icebergs?"

They bobbed below the pier.

Liam tossed his head back the way she'd seen

the surfers do, flinging the water out of his hair. "It's just right."

Felicia had done it.

She'd fallen.

She glanced upward. Anna was holding a camera over the edge of the rail.

Liam pointed under the pier. "Come on. Private spot."

He swam with strong strokes, and she dog-paddled behind him. At the third piling, he grabbed a metal bar. "Boat tie-up."

Instinctively, Felicia wrapped her arms around his neck. She was going for warmth at first, although his teeth were already chattering, too. She put her legs around him, too, and pulled him against her. "You have the funniest expression on your face."

Liam put his hands firmly at the small of her back. "I'd like to take this moment to remind you that shrinkage is a very real phenomenon. And I'm torn between wanting to swim straight to shore to warm up and kissing the hell out of you."

"Let's try that last one first." Felicia pressed her lips to his.

His lips were salty and ice-cold, the match to her own. His mouth, though, was a perfect heat, and she wanted to climb inside his skin. He clutched her hips and drew himself against her, and she could feel that shrinkage wasn't a *very* big issue. That, or her body heat was helping a little.

There was no way they could have sex in this ocean. They would die of hypothermia first.

But what a way to go.

Liam's mouth was as hard as the waves that were pushing them beachward, and his arms seemed as strong as the pier itself. Time stopped, just the way it had on the fall down to the water, but this time it wasn't because she was scared. She tightened her legs around his and felt as if she could hold on through anything that might come their way. "I'm a limpet." She laughed. "That didn't come out as sexy as I wanted it to."

He laughed and then shivered, a huge quake that she felt roll through her. The next wave pushed her sideways, breaking her clasp on him, and the piling scraped her shoulder. "Ooof."

"You're bleeding."

"I am? It doesn't hurt, though."

"That's pretty badass."

Pride filled her lungs. "It *is*."

"You're too numb to feel it yet. Let's head in before the sharks get the scent."

Every drop of blood in her body that had still had any lingering warmth went glacial. "Are you serious?"

"Eh, not really. It's been a long time since we've

seen any in these waters, and even longer since we've had a bite. They don't normally come in this close."

There was only one thing to say to that. "Race you back."

She left both him and her dog-paddle behind, drawing on the faster high school crawl she hadn't used in years.

And in her head, where normally she'd feel some kind of panic, she felt only excitement. She was on a date with a man who made her brave enough to leap from a pier *without* asking about sharks first.

There was a very good chance they'd both make it safe to shore.

And there was an even better chance that she'd be hopelessly in love with Liam by the time they got there.

THIRTY

The towels were waiting for them on the beach, and Felicia was glad. It was one thing to be naked in front of her staff on a pier with excitement coursing through her, and another thing to be naked while shaking and wet and almost-but-not-quite terrified. Her teeth chattered, and Anna had to help her get her dress over her head.

Liam was done dressing before she was, and looked even better post-dunking, if that was possible. His wet hair was slicked back, water still dripping to his shirt. His eyes blazed bright blue. Something about the jump had made him more comfortable in front of the cameras. "Are you ready for phase two of today's activities?"

"Does it involve heat of any sort?"

"Hot toddy?"

"Yes. Now, please."

"Come on, then. Just a short walk from here." He took her hand and Felicia shivered for the hundredth time, even though she wasn't cold anymore.

Caprese was one of the restaurants on the laminated sheet in her room at the Cat's Meow. "Elegant," she said. "I read they'll deliver you fresh garlic crab with enough notice."

"In season, they make a killing doing that. It's honestly just a fish joint, but it's our fish joint—Jake sells his catch here—so we like it."

Liam held open the door, and Felicia's stomach flipped. She was a feminist. If a man held open a door for her, she made a mental note to get his door next time. That was only fair.

But this was different. Something about the way Liam looked at her when he held open the door, the way he sheltered her body as she passed him, made her feel...safe. Cherished.

Was that what holding a door could mean? That you cherished someone?

Liam's gaze made her feel beautiful. Plain and simple.

The hostess seated them at a small table that stood against the glass window. The room itself was simple, decorated with red tablecloths and white candles. With its view, it didn't need more adornment. The restaurant sat on a platform over the water, and three glass walls let the marina view inside. Outside, yachts and catamarans bobbed next to bigger fishing trawlers. The last rays of the sun set lit the sky to the west, and the water was dark with pewter tips where the wind capped the waves.

Felicia fiddled with her napkin, tugging on the corner of it. When had she been on a date that mattered? Ever? Her only two long-term relationships had come out of friendships, and the dating had been casual at best. Felicia had never sat across the table from a man as handsome as Liam who wasn't either a studio executive or a hopeful actor.

And she'd never felt nerves like these, the ones that tingled down her arms all the way to her fingertips.

This could be the real thing. Or this could just be the fantasy.

The sheer contradiction of the two things made Felicia catch her breath. How could she have confused them for so long?

"You're gorgeous."

She believed him, that was the strange thing. She stretched her fingers out, and he caught her hands. "Well, you're amazing."

"It's like we're on television or something."

Oh, god.

For one wonderful second, she'd forgotten

about the camera crew. Sure, they'd followed them in, but Felicia was so used to being around their gear that somehow she'd forgotten *she* was the focus.

She and Liam.

They were actually creating the fantasy, building it. Women around the nation would sit cross-legged on their couches, chugging large glasses of red wine while wishing they were Felicia, that their husbands were Liam.

They were the fantasy, so what did that mean?

Felicia took her hands back and opened the menu, but her brain forgot how to read. She studied each line carefully, absorbing not a single appetizer or entrée.

If they were the fantasy, then it logically followed that they weren't the real thing.

Nothing was as good as the fantasy. Real life was a disappointment—always. That's the way the world worked. And on-screen lives—the lives she filmed—those she could control. Those were feelings she could work with so they didn't threaten to rise up and swamp her, taking her down to the bottom. Earlier, she'd popped to the surface of the ocean, but that was because Liam had been beside her.

Liam leaned forward. "What is going on in your

head right now? Is the menu that bad? Do you not like fish?"

"What are we doing?" She gestured around the empty dining room. The network had bought out the room, like it always did. It wouldn't do to have a cackling tourist wearing a tacky shirt in the background. "This is ridiculous."

"Talk to me."

She couldn't. This was her job, to create and maintain a dream world, one that people who didn't have family could escape into. So she just shook her head. She closed her eyes, and imagined she could feel the building rocking in the waves underneath them.

"What are you feeling?"

Had he felt it, too? Her eyes flew open. "Is the building actually moving?" Or was she now imagining things, the feeling of her moorings loosening, drifting?

Liam smiled. "It rocks a little bit when the bigger waves hit. But that's not what I meant. What are you feeling about this? About us?"

"I can't—we should just figure out what we want to eat." They could edit this part out later. All they really needed on film were a few seconds in this restaurant, a couple of smiles. That would be enough to frost the dream cupcake.

"I want to do this with you."

"Good. I'm glad. It's going to be a good show." Felicia could be polite all night. She could cry later.

"No." He glanced to the left at Tony, and then shook his head, as if trying to forget he'd looked. "I want to do *all* of this with you. I don't want this to be about just the house of your dreams. I want this..."

He drew a deep breath, and Felicia felt her own chest rise to match it.

"I don't care that we're on TV. I would want this no matter what. From the moment I first saw you in my kitchen, confused by the sight of a peanut butter and jelly sandwich, I haven't been able to think about anything else except seeing you again. I know it's too soon, and too fast, and I know that were on national television right now, but we weren't the other night."

In her peripheral vision, Felicia saw Anna shoot a look at Tony.

No, they couldn't know about the other night. That was theirs alone. "Liam—I know that—"

"I'm falling in love with you. And I'm terrified that you're going to say that this is only about the house, only about the show. I'm terrified that..." He looked down at his salad fork.

He was terrified that he wasn't lovable enough. She could see it in the tension in his eyes, in the way his body seemed ready for flight.

She was falling, too.

She was falling so damn hard. But she couldn't say it, couldn't spit it out in front of the cameras. It wouldn't be *real* if she said it while she was on the clock.

It wasn't fair—he'd set his heart between them on the table as if it were an amuse-bouche, and it sat there, beating so loudly she could almost hear it. She had to tell him how she felt—but that would be *admitting* she felt it—and she should do it fast—but the cameras were watching, and she wanted it to be real.

But the cameras couldn't see under the table.

She stealthily eased her foot free from one pump and slid her bare toes under his pants leg. The questioning look didn't leave his face, but some of the tension melted from his shoulders.

A cell phone rang. Liam jumped and reached in his coat pocket. "I put it on silent, but Timbo can always ring through. I'm just going to get this real quick." He hurried toward the front door, the phone at his ear. Tony followed.

Anna took the opportunity to scurry forward. "This is amazing. Is this scripted? Because I honestly can't tell."

Felicia shook her head, still unable to speak.

"Whatever it is, it's filming great. Like, *On the Market* is going to be *huge*. Hashtag Team Liam. I can see it now. Whatever you and Natasha cooked up, I approve. This is good shit." Anna glanced at her iPad. "Speaking of her, she's been blowing up my phone. Have you checked yours?"

"No."

"Maybe you should."

Felicia checked her cell. Four missed calls and twelve texts, all from Natasha. Quickly, she swiped through the texts.

I need you here.

Drop what you're doing. The Allens talked, even with the NDA.

The Allens were a couple from their reality wedding series—if they went public with how much they were paid to sleep in the same bed, even after John Allen's affair—it wouldn't look good for the network. It was currently their biggest money-maker, and they couldn't lose that.

Felicia swiped to the next message.

If we slap them with a lawsuit fast enough, we might get them to shut up, but I think it's too late.

Felicia's head started to ache.

Dammit, answer me!

First plane, get on it. I'm not kidding.

She was getting nauseated.

We can reshoot whatever it is you're doing. That show doesn't matter, not right now. Get here.

In the corner of her eye, she saw Liam hurrying

back through the empty dining room. His brows were drawn together, his gait quick.

Felicia placed her cell face down on the table, her fingers icy. "Are you all right?"

"I hate to do this, but Timbo's gotten himself arrested. I have to rain check this, and I hate that so much that it hurts."

"It's fine. Go." She should tell him she had to fly to LA. She should tell him so much more than that. But there wasn't time.

Liam stooped and kissed her. It was fast and light, a goodbye kiss.

"Bye," was all she said. She kept her hand on top of her phone until he was gone, as if it were a poisonous insect she had to protect him from.

Her heart hurt. Ached, actually, with something she didn't—couldn't—name.

Then she picked up her cell and started texting back.

THIRTY-ONE

"Arrested." Liam didn't know when he'd been more disappointed, and he was sure at least eighty percent of it was because of Timbo's actions, not because he'd had to leave Felicia behind at the restaurant.

"It's not that big of a deal." Timbo kept his face pointed out the car window, so Liam couldn't tell what his expression was.

"You got arrested for graffiti. You know what that looks like on the record of a boy like you?"

"A boy like me? Really?" Timbo turtled his neck and hunched into his hoodie.

"You *know* you have to consider what the rest of the world thinks. They look at your skin color, they'll think you're trouble. You have a greater chance of getting pulled over, of getting shot. Every time you leave the house, I worry."

"It was just some tagging. I'll clean it off."

Anger rose in Liam, and he clutched the steering wheel more tightly. "That's the point, you don't get to just clean this one up and get away with it. A penis on her garage door, really? Mrs. Doyle wants to prosecute."

A shrug was his answer.

"That doesn't freak you out?"

"It's a misdemeanor. I'm a minor. No big."

Liam yanked the wheel and pulled in the driveway. The fact that Timbo knew both of those things infuriated him. A kid shouldn't know that a misdemeanor wasn't a big deal, and a kid shouldn't know that his under-eighteen records would eventually be sealed. But kids knew that today, even the good ones.

And god bless it, Timbo was one of the good ones. He was a freaking great one. But all it took was one wrong step, and he'd be right on the path his mother took before him. Liam knew there was nothing down that path but heartbreak, and he sure as hell didn't want to watch the boy he loved fall down it.

His phone rang. He didn't recognize the number, but it was probably something about Timbo. "Go inside. We'll talk more in a minute."

Timbo slammed the car door behind him. No surprise there.

"Hello?"

"Liam? This is Natasha Nguyen, from the network."

Good grief, had he blown the whole show by leaving the date? For a second he remembered Felicia's face as he told her he was falling in love with her. He could've sworn she was close to saying something similar back to him. "It was a family emergency. I couldn't get out of it, but I swear to you I'm still very much interested in the project. My brothers and I all are. We're taking it very seriously."

Her voice filled his speakers over the car's Bluetooth. "Oh, you didn't do a thing wrong. On the contrary. I'm calling to apologize to you for ripping our Felicia away from you so unceremoniously. I have a major fire, and she's the only one good enough to help me put it out. I'll only need to borrow her for a few days, a week at the most."

"I'm confused. Felicia's where?" It hadn't even been two hours since he got the call from Sheriff McMurtry.

"She's already in the air, I'm afraid. She asked me to send you her apologies."

"Of course. But—"

"The show goes on, and I'm sorry for that. We'll have the camera crew in with your brothers as they complete the work this week, but what I need from you is a little bit bigger."

How bad was this going to be? "Yeah?"

"Since we didn't get enough footage today of your date, I need a reassurance from you that you'd be comfortable being filmed with Felicia in the future."

None of this made sense. "I don't get it."

"I'm sorry, I'm not being clear. Felicia has made it clear to me that she's legitimately interested in you. To be honest, this kind of boggles my mind – she's married to her work, and that's what I love about her. What I'm hoping to hear from you is that you wouldn't mind re-creating some scenes with her, to fill in the blanks. It's a short episode, we don't need many more. Maybe just a couple."

All Liam could focus on was that his hunch—his hope—was confirmed. *Legitimately interested.* It wasn't very romantic, but it sure as hell would do. "Of course, whatever you all need from me, I'm happy to do."

A light tinkle of laughter filled his car. "I'm so relieved to hear you say that. Before Felicia gets back, I'd love to get a couple of diary cams filmed. I loved the first one you did—"

"Excuse me?"

"You know, the one where you said you weren't lovable. I don't know if you're naïve or a genius, and I don't care. The more unlovable you say you are on screen, the more lovable it automatically makes you."

Liam's throat itched. "That was supposed to be erased."

"Erased?" Natasha laughed again. "Oh, no, darling, that would be terrible. It's gold, I'm surprised Felicia didn't tell you that."

"I'm not—"

"But really, what I'm looking for is just a touch more. If we could get you on camera looking emotionally vulnerable, that would be amazing. And I know it doesn't all come down to money, but cash is king, I find."

"I have no idea what you're talking about."

"I'm offering you ten thousand more to talk on camera about your parents wanting nothing to do with you." The mirth was gone from her voice.

She was actually fucking serious.

And that wasn't the worst part. "Felicia told you about that?" When? That very night? While he'd slept naked on the sofa and she'd worked, literally still lying in his arms?

"Don't be mad at her, that's her job. She gets me the goods, and I make them *really* good. I squeeze the juice out. Abandoned by your parents *and* by your fiancé—the whole world will love you."

If Jake found out that their father hadn't wanted him—if Aidan found out that their mother had been going to leave him behind—it was unthinkable. And if they knew *no one* had wanted Liam, they'd be devastated on his behalf. They'd be outraged. He'd never told a single soul. Bill had been the only one who'd known, and Liam had been planning on taking it to his grave, just like Bill had. "No."

"Twenty thousand."

"This isn't up for discussion."

"Twenty-five, but I swear to god I can't go higher. I've already spent too much on this show."

Liam heard a sharp crack. In his left hand he held the turn signal, which he'd somehow snapped off, without trying. He let it go, and it dangled from its interior wire.

"Liam?"

"I can't believe she told you."

"Think about it, okay? I'll call you again tomorrow. And I said I couldn't go higher, but if you throw in the part about your foster kid having the same kind of parents you did, I'll come up with an all-expenses Disney cruise for you and the kid and your brothers and whoever else you want to bring."

There was a quick buzz, and then empty silence.

Liam held his hands in front of him. He looked at the backs of them and then turned them slowly so he was looking at the palms. Both of his brothers had been in plenty of fights growing up, and not just with each other. They'd fought on the playground, and more than once they'd fought as men, usually for stupid reasons. Liam had punched Aidan in the ear when he was fourteen, but he hadn't been drawn to violence since.

Now, he felt like hitting something. Anything. If he'd had a punching bag, he would have bloodied his hands on it. He considered going to the Golden Spike and seeing if he could nudge Damien Scandi into anger. Damien Scandi *always* wanted to fight someone.

Felicia had asked him, point blank, to tell her his biggest fear. He had. And he'd told her the why behind it.

Then Felicia had told a woman who would tell the rest of the world.

It was his own damn fault. He'd walked himself into the trap. Maybe he'd sensed that Felicia was bait at that first kiss—maybe that's why he'd thrown himself over the balcony to get away from her.

Her job was to get the goods for Natasha.

He wondered what Felicia got paid. Undoubtedly she was the highest-paid actress who wasn't an actress in Hollywood.

Had she even *wanted* the house?

Had she made up the dream house she'd told him about?

The thought that she might have lied about even that, from the very beginning, was unbearable.

Liam pulled out the keys and gripped them so hard he set off the emergency alarm. He punched at the buttons to silence the noise.

The night they'd spent together. They'd struck the contact clause from his contract, but what about her contract? Did *she* get a nice big bonus for sleeping with him?

Liam got out of the car and looked up into the blackness. Darling Bay was socked in tonight, and he could hear the foghorn mourning in the distance. It would've been a perfect night to walk her back to the Cat's Claw, to wrap his arms around her, to kiss her good night and promise her his tomorrow. And the next one, and the one after that.

He reached down and picked up a stone. Then he hurled it at the stop sign, something he'd told Timbo not to do again and again. It hit the dented sign with a satisfying thwack.

And if he hit it a thousand more times, if he crushed it with a boulder, it still wouldn't erase the word he should've heeded the first time he saw her:

STOP. Stop hoping, stop dreaming, stop wishing he was someone else, someone different, someone better. He'd been getting along just fine.

Alone.

He'd just go back to being happy that way.

Somehow.

THIRTY-TWO

After two eighteen-hour days, Felicia had tidied most of the legal problems. The Allens had needed diligent finessing, but their show would be better than ever now that Mrs. Allen was not only pregnant with a child that wasn't her husband's, but that she was willing to talk about it on camera.

Felicia put her head back, and looked up at the ceiling. Her office was well appointed with elegant furnishing in dark blues and browns that had taken two design committees to decide upon. She spent more time here than she'd ever spent in her place. Truthfully, her condo had never felt like home. If anything, this office—full of books and scripts and awards and changes of clothes and her favorite prints on the walls and the couch perfect for napping on—was the only place she felt at home in LA.

And her office was a hundred percent different from the treehouse, with its ramshackle flooring and tilting walls and the smell of resin and bark and wind. The only place she'd ever felt truly at *home*.

She wanted to go back to Darling Bay.

To Liam.

She looked through her missed phone calls, and there were a lot of them. She'd put her phone on silent for the last five hours while she finished up the last of her work. If she hadn't, nothing would have gotten done. And in the back of her mind, she hoped that if he couldn't get through to her, *that* would be the time he called. He would finally return one of her texts or one of her emails.

But there was nothing from him.

It was almost midnight, way too late to call anyone. Too late even to text. Her heart clunked in her chest, sounding like the broken wind chime on Liam's porch. Tired, and tied up in knots.

Why hadn't he called her back?

What if something was really wrong with Timbo? Wouldn't Liam have been able to find a minute or two to shoot her a message? Isn't that what most people would have done?

But what if he didn't *want* her to come back? The brave part of her heart wanted to roll into the shape of a fiddlehead fern, tucked away and safe from pain.

There was a sharp rap at her door, and Natasha stuck her head in. "All done?"

"Yep." Felicia scrambled to grab her purse, to make it look as if she'd been about to head out. "On my way home to grab a few winks."

"You really saved my ass on this. I owe you."

No, she didn't. Natasha paid her debts with bonuses, money that could be tracked, favors with receipts. Natasha owed Felicia nothing except a glowing letter of reference if she....

If she quit? The idea flitted through her head for the first time. It was a disloyal thought, but it was one she wanted to pull out and look at later, when she was alone. Quitting wasn't something she ever thought she would do. This job had meant everything to Felicia. When had that changed? When had *she* changed?

Natasha was staring at her, her head tilted to the side. Felicia realized she hadn't answered her. "You don't owe me a thing, you know that."

"You okay? You seem a little off."

"Just tired. So I'll see you tomorrow, okay?"

"Before you go, would you mind looking at the diary cam we just got from Liam?"

"You've been talking to him?" The pain that

had been lurking behind Felicia's left eye got sharper.

"Anna has. I took a look at it, and I've got to be honest with you, I was hoping for better. From what you told me, I thought we'd get something dirtier, something juicier from him. What he sent was a little too sweet for my taste. Made my cavities hurt. But what do I know? I'm so tired I can't see straight. We did a test viewing, and the audience loved him, so you can't ask for more than that." Natasha shot her a look she couldn't parse. "They didn't like you much, but that's okay. You're not the reason they'll tune into the next episode."

"They didn't like me?" For some reason it stung. She'd never wanted to be in front of the camera, but once she'd gotten there, she'd hoped she would be okay. Acceptable.

"Just watch it before you go home. Let me know in the morning what you think."

THIRTY-THREE

No one was in the editing bay, which was just as well. Lily and Gomez tended to be so proprietary over their work they wouldn't let anyone else even push a button. Felicia had started in editing a long time ago. Things had changed, but not that much. It felt good to be in the edit chair again.

Maybe she should never have climbed the management ladder.

If she hadn't, maybe she'd be married with babies, living in the Valley in a brand-new four-thousand square foot house that smelled like new carpet and room fragrance spray.

If she hadn't, would she ever have found her way to Darling Bay?

She found the segment from Anna, and hit play.

Liam's face filled the screen. The look of him hit her like a punch to the stomach. She'd *missed* him. She'd been gone for less than a week. She shouldn't miss anyone this much. A smile spread across her face as she listened. She couldn't help hoping—desperately—that he'd mention her, that he'd been missing her, too.

But his face was serious, his eyebrows drawn together, his lips thin. Did he look pale? "Yeah, I've been thinking a lot about what home means to me. I love my house. You've seen it, that old Victorian with my office in the front, and a messy kitchen and living room in the back. Timbo's bedroom is upstairs, and mine is down the hall. It's a good place, and I'm happy to have it." Liam's gaze went downward as if he were holding something just out of sight of the camera. "But a house doesn't matter, does it? What matters are the people who make our lives worth living."

Felicia's heart pounded harder. People like him made life worth living. Liam—*he* was the reason she needed to get back to Darling Bay. Not the treehouse, even though she yearned for it. Yearning was just an intense want. She could handle that just fine. She'd watched television and yearned for her own fantasy come true all her life.

What she *couldn't* handle for much longer was this need. She needed to be with Liam like she needed air.

What if she quit?

What would she do next?

She knew almost without thinking. If she quit, she'd cash out some stocks and build a portfolio of clients she might be able to work for remotely, and she'd move to Darling Bay permanently.

Liam. How could she miss a person she hadn't even known existed until less than two months ago? Feeling silly and small and hopelessly excited, Felicia bit her bottom lip and kept watching.

Liam looked straight into the camera. He was getting so much better at that. "Sometimes, I guess I wondered if I was unlovable, because my parents left. But me and my brothers, we had Bill. He loved us better than our own flesh and blood ever could have. He adopted us, and we took his last name. We'll always be the Ballard Brothers, and I'm pretty excited to announce right here and now, that the adoption paperwork for my foster son Timbo has gone through. Real soon he'll be a Ballard boy, too. Love always get its way, even if it goes a roundabout way to get there. Sometimes it takes someone important letting you down to make you see who's still there, who's really important. And we Ballard men don't need anyone but ourselves."

Something cold and heavy sunk into the pit of Felicia's stomach.

He knew.

He knew she'd told Natasha about his backstory. Felicia felt as if she were falling off the pier all over again, but alone this time. Who had told him? Natasha herself? Anna?

There was a break in the film, and Anna's voice could be heard in the background. It would be edited out when the show was put together. "What about Felicia?"

"Felicia?" Liam's eyes were iceberg blue. "Yeah. I guess we had a good time, and I wish her the best in her new house. I have to say, I enjoyed my time in her treehouse. And, hell." Liam leaned back and grinned at the camera. "If she's an example of the kind of woman y'all pick for us to date, then this show is just going to keep getting better and better. I can't wait to meet the next one."

Felicia hit stop.

Stop.

Her hopes crashed to the ground, shattering at her feet. The ice she'd seen in his eyes had frozen her blood.

She'd done this to him. It didn't matter who had told Liam that she'd divulged his secret heart. He knew, that's all that mattered. Liam knew that Felicia had exposed him, and she knew he wouldn't forgive her.

Behind her, someone moved in the dark.

Felicia spun.

Natasha took a step forward into the light. "Yeah, that's my fault. I told him that I wanted to use it on film, and he shut down."

"I told him we wouldn't use it. That no one would see it."

"That was dumb."

"I was in love with him." The pain of the words set her throat on fire. Tears would have helped, if she'd been able to remember where they lived inside her body.

"We can get you out of the house contract. We'll have the studio take over the rest of the paperwork, and as soon as it's in your name, we can turn around and resell."

Felicia stared at this woman she barely recognized.

"Or, if you're willing to wait a little while... They've already done the renovations, and all we need from you is a quick walk-through with Aidan. Liam doesn't even need to be there. Then the show'll be in the can, and the second it hits primetime, the asking price will shoot up."

"Are you actually serious?"

Natasha just raised an eyebrow, something that Felicia used to be afraid of.

"You want me to go back up there? On camera?"

"Of course I do."

"Did you hear what I said, about love? Do you need me to define the word? Have you been here so long you've forgotten what's possible? What's important?"

Natasha folded her arms. "Honey. I know you're mad at me. But we can get through this. Don't forget you love your job. This is what you *do*. This is who we are."

It wasn't just that she felt trapped, she *was* trapped. Felicia was walled in by the paperwork she herself had helped draft, the contracts she'd signed of her own volition. The network's legal team went to sleep dreaming about these kinds of problems.

"I quit." The two words were so simple to say, and felt so good in her mouth, that Felicia wondered why she waited so long to see them. Natasha just shook her head. "You can't quit."

Panic beat in Felicia's chest for the space of the breath, and then she realized she didn't have to explain it to Natasha. She didn't owe an explanation to anyone.

Except to Liam, and he probably didn't want to hear it. She certainly wouldn't, if she were him.

"I'll fulfill my contract. I'm giving you thirty days' notice, and I'll film the last segment with Aidan. The house is mine to sell, not the network's." And she *would* sell it. How could she live there, remembering their night under the redwood's branches?

"You're actually serious?"

Felicia would work out the rest of her contract, but no more diary cams. Her throat was barely keeping back the tears—she just had to get out of this studio and into her sterile condo, where she could get under the covers and cry for the next three years or so.

She picked up both her bags and put the straps over her shoulders. "His last diary cam is perfect. The audience will love it. Well done." She walked past Natasha, whose mouth was still hanging open.

Felicia left the lot and walked toward her car, trailing her broken heart behind her like a ripped, dirty blanket that would never keep her warm again.

THIRTY-FOUR

Liam had done his level goddamn best to get out of the filmed last walk-through, but Aidan wasn't having it. "Me and Jake did every single bit of the work in this place while you moped and whined for the last week. You don't have to talk to her. I don't care if you even look at her, but you better be there with us for the reveal."

Timbo, the traitor, nodded along with Aidan. "I'll tag her car while you're going through the house if it makes you feel better."

Liam glared at Timbo. "You so much as touch a spray paint can in the next five years, and I'll make you sleep under a bridge."

Timbo grinned. Since the adoption papers

came through the week before, the kid had changed. He'd finally unpacked the one box he'd arrived with, putting his books and softballs and various Pez dispensers on the shelves in his room. He experimented once with calling Liam *Dad*, and then both of them had gone red. It would probably stick, though. Or at least, Liam hoped it would.

Now, as the Liam pulled up to the old Maupin property, his heart clapped around the interior of his chest like a broken dinner bell. Not much noise, but damn uncomfortable.

This was the reveal. His job was to let Felicia into her new house.

Her new house in Darling Bay. Her new home was in *his* hometown, and while Liam knew he'd never move away, he couldn't quite imagine staying, either.

At least he'd gotten used to the bustle of the all the motion on set. He counted at least four cameramen heading toward the house, and another couple of them going inside. The boom mics swung like gigantic cat toys overhead. Anna saw him coming and raised a hand. "Have you seen what your brothers did inside?"

"They haven't let me look." It wasn't totally true —they'd wanted him to see, but he'd refused to make the drive. The only way to recover from the tsunami that had ruined his quiet, happy life was to avoid the wreckage it had left in its wake.

"You're going to love it. Oh, there she is now."

He heard car tires crunching up the driveway behind him.

Two cameras focused on him, one on either side, and he remembered again how much he hated the feel of that gaze. The cameras were silent, and they weren't even that close, but they represented millions of Americans, all of whom would have opinions about who Liam was. And not one of them would know that Liam Ballard was a man hopelessly in love with a woman who had betrayed him for her job.

He would make sure it stayed that way, too.

"So here you go, moment of truth." God, he hated what he'd done, the sentimentality he allowed himself to feel when making this last gift for her. Whatever. *Give it to her, let her have it, and be done with her.* "Your key."

He handed it to her. She took the long silver chain, and stared at the key that hung from it.

"That looks like—" Felicia's eyes swung to meet his. "Liam. Is this my key?"

"You'll never know until you try it in the door." He tried to insert a smile into his voice, since it wasn't rising all the way to his face.

For a second, it looked as if she'd try to push the question further, but then she turned to the door and slid the key inside. With a *snick*, the door opened smoothly into the kitchen.

Aidan, Jake, and Timbo waited for her, and applauded as she made her way inside. There were more camera people then there were normal people, and Liam ducked backward quietly. This was her time, not his. He had done his part.

A hundred feet from the driveway stood an ancient oak tree with limbs that seemed to spread forever. Where the redwood in the heart of Felicia's house went up, this oak went out. An old wooden swing hung from a thick branch. It would be as good a place as any to wait for Timbo to be done.

Liam sat carefully, testing the ropes for weakness. They creaked, but they held his weight.

Wouldn't it be nice, if a person could test the heart the same way? The ropes around his weren't strong enough to hold the pain of Felicia for much longer. Maybe he'd go on vacation for a few weeks, him and Timbo fishing down in Catalina, or maybe a backpacking trip into the Sierras. Anything to get Liam out and away from the woman who starred in his daydreams and walked through his dreams at night. Every night.

Sunlight filtered through the oak leaves, falling

on his shoulders. The air smelled like dust and wood and warm rosemary. It would be the kind of evening that begged for a barbecue and a cold beer on a porch.

Felicia had that porch now. It was all hers. Liam knew that Aidan had extended the second-floor porch so that a set of stairs led right up to the treehouse platform. No more rickety ladder.

Who would sit up there with her? Who would watch the incremental growth of the tree's trunk over the years? Who would remember what the place had looked like when it was sad and abandoned? Now it was bright and airy and perfect for a woman like Felicia.

Sometimes Liam forgot that she'd just been doing her job. Sometimes he wondered when she was coming home, for real. For good.

He looked up at the treehouse's high platform, and as if he'd conjured her, there she was. No one else, no cameras around her. She must have fobbed them off, and he was sure they were filming from the bottom of the stairs. But no one was with her as she raised her hand to her lips. Then she held her hand out, and blew.

She blew a kiss to him.

And, goddammit, it hit him like a cannonball.

It wasn't fair. It wasn't right. He jumped off the

swing, and headed for his car. He'd send a text to Aidan to bring Timbo home when they were done.

He didn't have to put up with this.

Actually, he couldn't.

It was enough that his heart was broken, but for her to witness the damage was unthinkable.

THIRTY-FIVE

Felicia watched him drive away without surprise. She didn't know why she'd blown the kiss. It had probably seemed as if she were rubbing salt in his wound. As if she'd been out to get him this way the whole time.

Nothing was further from the truth. It had been a real kiss. A true one.

But she'd lost the chance to tell him anything true at all.

From below, came Timbo's voice calling up to her. "Do you like it?"

She climbed down the steps.

Timbo was jumping up and down on the newly refinished hardwood floors. "So, what? Are you surprised? Do you love it all?" One of the cameras was trained on him, but he didn't seem to notice at all. "Is it what you wanted? Did we do a good job?"

The answers to those questions were simple. Yes, she loved it, and yes, she was surprised at how much work Aidan and Jack had done while she was working her last thirty days finishing up her job in LA. The rusted cast-iron clawfoot tub had been replaced with a solid spa tub in gorgeous shape, so sturdy it would outlive them all. They'd redone the parlor exactly as she'd wanted—still full of companionable furniture and a few new, more modern pieces, it also featured the stag-hunting rug, which had been cleaned and fixed and was even more impressive.

And the green sofa.

That damned green sofa.

"I love every single thing about it."

Timbo beamed, and Aidan nodded as if he wasn't surprised. Jake shot her a smile, and then went back to flirting quietly with the new girl in Production. Felicia hadn't caught her name, and now, she supposed, she'd never have to know it.

"Where did Liam go?"

Aidan glanced sideways at her. "Probably to pull more comps, now that your house has brought them up. Never stops working. And I know he's already hunting for a showstopper like this one.

Wants to make the network happy, and keep the bucks rolling in."

Anna arranged them all on the front steps, and one of the cameras pulled back far enough to get the whole redwood in the shot. She was doing her job well, taking every extra little step that would be noticed by Natasha, in the hopes she'd get Felicia's job. She probably would. And she'd be good at it, maybe better than Felicia had been. It didn't hurt to think about.

Anna scowled and looked at her iPad. "Liam should be here. Didn't we get that in his contract, that he has to follow through?"

"Don't worry." Felicia knew that Liam's not being in this shot would read as mysterious. "You can make me the bad guy, blame me for quitting my job and pissing him off. Make me the villain. It'll just make him look better to the rest of the world."

Anna shot her a look of gratefulness. "I have no idea what we're going to do without you."

"You won't even notice I'm gone." Felicia knew it was true—in two weeks, they'd all remember Felicia as a hard worker, and that was about it. Everyone was replaceable. "You know, if you put me on the bottom step, the light will fall better on Aidan and Jake." This was her last moment, but it was really the beginning for them.

In the signature phrase decided on by Natasha

and two of her creatives, Felicia had to deliver the last lines of the show. "I had a great time dating Liam Ballard, but he and his brothers are still on the market." She patted the railing. "But not this house. It's off the market, and it's all mine."

All hers.

Once she sold it, what would she have left? The condo in LA that was never home? She had no interest in going back there. Under her fingertips, the wood felt solid. Strong. The way she wanted to feel someday.

Anna and the crew got some final shots before wrapping set. Aidan and Jake collected their tools and Timbo poked at gopher holes near the oak tree.

And Felicia wondered what would happen if she *didn't* sell.

If she put down roots here, how would she grow? Could she, so close to Liam?

She remembered the key on the silver chain. Now that she wasn't on camera, she could take a moment to inspect it, to prove her hunch had been wrong.

But when she held it in the light and tilted it, there it was. In tiny letters was stamped *HOME.*

The ache behind her eyes grew sharper, and her vision blurred with tears that rose hot and insistent. This was her key. No wonder she thought she'd lost it forever. He'd taken it and had it recut to fit the door of her dreams. No one had ever given her a sweeter gift.

Soon she'd be able to go inside—into her own home, not the Cat's Claw—and climb up to the treehouse and cry for as long as she had tears in her body, which might end up being forever. But right now, she needed to do something else.

"Anna?"

Anna was breaking down a jib arm. "Yeah?"

"Have you packed up the diary cam yet? I need one more take."

THIRTY-SIX

The last time Liam had been inside the Golden Spike, he'd gotten so drunk he'd met a network executive and pitched her a television show which turned out to be one of his least good ideas, ever.

This time, he wasn't going to have as much vodka, that was for sure. No matter what his brothers tried to say about it.

Norma was in her regular spot at the bar near the door. She was laying out tarot cards and trying to talk two tourists into paying her for a reading. "Come on, don't you want to know when you'll meet the man of your dreams?" Her necklaces jangled and her eyes crossed slightly as she tapped the back of the deck. The women were already reaching for their wallets.

Nate Houston and Adele Darling were tending bar, and Adele's sister Molly was dancing with the sheriff to an old country tune playing on the jukebox. Four old men played poker in the corner, pretending they weren't playing with cash, hiding the singles badly under coasters every time the sheriff glanced their way.

It could have been any other night in the Golden Spike, but Adele had promised this one would be special.

And by special she must have meant especially awful. "We have to celebrate the first episode! Everyone will be there, and you have to be, too."

He'd begged off, citing Timbo as the reason he wouldn't be able to attend. Adele might want a viewing party, but she wasn't going to let a minor into her bar, not even for a special occasion. But then she'd gone and hired a damn babysitter and opened up the apartment over the bar. "We'll do a MythBusters marathon, and I'll provide all the pizza and ice cream they can scarf up. Anybody who wants to drop their kids up there, can. We'll drink downstairs and laugh at you Ballard boys. God knows the Darling Songbirds have gotten enough attention in this town." Adele threw a wink at her sister Molly. "It's time we let you guys have some of it. Channel 2 said they'd be here to get your reaction."

Fantastic. More on-camera time.

The problem was, the check had come. Not only had it been bigger than they'd planned, but it hadn't bounced. They were so close to opening Ballard Youth that they could almost taste it. They still needed a building, but the funds were there. In place. The town's goodwill would go a long way to getting the zoning when they needed it. Showing up at a town party in honor of him and his brothers was the least he could do.

Even though the thought of seeing Felicia on a big screen kind of made him want to hurl.

Felicia.

It'd been five weeks since he'd seen her at the house, since she'd blown him that terrible, beautiful kiss. Every day he scanned the MLS, and every day her house wasn't listed. Timbo said he thought he'd seen her at Martha's Market, but he also thought he'd seen Van Damme surfing, so he wasn't the most reliable eyewitness.

Liam hadn't known it was possible to miss someone as much as he missed Felicia. He definitely had never missed Brandy this way.

Talking to Felicia had felt like finally being understood in his native tongue, as if he'd been struggling with a language, and then he'd been allowed to relax. Being with her had felt like being in the home he'd always wanted. It had nothing to do with wood or brick or plaster—it had to do with her. Who she was.

Felicia had texted him at least five times. *Call me. Please just call me back.*

She'd emailed him. *We need to talk. Please.*

She'd even come by the office once. Timbo said she'd left in a hurry when he told her Liam wasn't home.

She'd only called him one time, and the sight of her name on the screen of his cell had made his hand shake. He had just decided to answer—what the hell?—when it had stopped ringing.

Since then, she hadn't tried to contact him at all.

Just as well.

She'd screwed up. He'd told his deepest secret to someone who had the power to share it with the whole world, the power to hurt his brothers. And she'd promised to protect that secret.

That was the other reason he was here tonight. If his brothers heard the truth about their parents from a goddamn television show, then at least Liam would be in the room to smash his fist through the bar's brand-new big-screen TV. Then the sheriff could haul him out, but at least he'd be there to apologize to his brothers, to beg one of them to watch Timbo until he got home. On second thought, social services probably wouldn't think much of a new adoptive father committing vandalism, the crime he was supposed to be keeping Timbo from repeating. Shit.

His brothers arrived at the bar, Aidan covered in sawdust and scowling, Jake smiling like he'd just slept all day in the sun, which he probably had. Good-natured ribbing followed, and Liam put on the smile he'd have to keep plastered on until the end of the night. No matter what. More townsfolk arrived, and laughter rose through the room.

The show started, and Adele turned up the TV's volume. When the first shot of the three brothers filled the screen, the entire bar cheered loud enough to wake old Hugh Darling who was sleeping in the cemetery up the road.

Then Felicia came on screen. She ducked through the small round door into the kitchen, Liam on her heels. God, look at his face. He'd been so into her, even then. He hadn't even known. Maybe he should feel embarrassed, but he didn't, not really. He just wanted to keep watching her.

He realized the bar had quieted. When he looked around, all eyes were on him. "What?" he said loudly. "You think just because we didn't end up together I regret doing this? Marcie Deakin was the top realtor in this area until tonight, but I bet I outsell her this next year." Marcie protested loudly and the bar's patrons relaxed into laughter.

Liam settled onto the barstool that had been saved for him and took a long sip of his beer. This would be agony, surgery without anesthesia, and then it would be over, and he could restart his life. Somehow. For a moment he tried to imagine Darling Bay with her in it. Felicia Turbinado, a local. He imagined waving to her as he passed.

No.

He and Timbo would just have to move, that was all. And his brothers. And the whole town, if it came to that. They'd uproot everything but the Maupin house (the Turbinado house now) and start over, two hundred miles north, where the land was more rugged and the wind colder but at least Felicia wouldn't be nearby.

Speaking of her, the whole bar watched Felicia explore the house. They watched her expression as she took the steps up to the platform above. She'd done a good job pretending it was her first time inside, her first time climbing the ladder. But then again, she really *had* been that excited every time.

The network had sent Liam an early digital copy of the show. He hadn't been able to watch it— he hadn't wanted to know ahead of time just how bad it was going to be. But now he was glad. If he wanted to—and he would—he could watch and re-watch just that section. Her climbing the ladder, her laughter filtering down to him.

Aidan nudged his elbow. "You ever going to tell us what happened?"

Liam shushed him. A diary cam part was starting. This would be when everything fell apart.

Above their heads, the big-screen Liam spoke. "I guess you would say my last relationship was heartbreaking. And it was. My heart broke when she didn't show up for the wedding rehearsal. But then I got over it."

The camera cut to Jake, who was sawing a piece of wood. "Nah, my brother's tough. When my parents took off, it was him who took care of us. Bill Ballard was a good man, and we're proud to have his name. But my big brother did more than anyone else to make sure we were raised right." On screen, Jake scratched his nose. "When's my turn, anyway? Will I get to pick the girl?"

Bar patrons laughed. Someone clapped Liam on the back. Jake clinked shots with someone, and Aidan whooped.

Liam stared up at the screen, unable to believe it. During the commercial break, people tried to chat with him. He ignored them. He kept his eyes on the screen, ready for the moment he saw himself admit on national television he was unlovable, prepped for the moment Felicia broke the news that their parents had only wanted one or two of the boys—and that no one had wanted Liam.

Then it was almost over. On screen, they showed the kiss that came right before their jump from the pier. His buttocks gleamed white, but they'd tastefully blurred Felicia's nethers.

A quick shot of them swimming to shore. Another shot of them in candlelight, laughing.

Then Liam watched a pale version of himself handing Felicia a key. Her face went so bright it hurt to look at her.

They'd caught the kiss she threw him from the top of the tree house.

They'd caught his expression, too. The one that said he was brokenhearted.

In the bar, Liam felt his face go red. He'd never felt so exposed. Jake leaned against his shoulder for a moment, silently propping him up.

The theme music swelled.

Felicia came back on screen, but she looked different. She'd already done a couple of diary cams, innocuous things about what her dream kitchen might look like, and how she worked too much to really date at home in LA. This was different. Her nose was red, and her eyes glistened. Her expression was dead serious, not a glint of humor dancing across her face.

"I'm pretty sure a lot of people will ask me how I let someone like Liam go. The answer to that is we let each other go. He saw me for me, and it's been forever since someone did that." She tried to smile, but it wobbled. "I saw him as the man he is, gentle, generous, incredibly hot—"

The bar patrons whooped.

"—kind, and caring. I fell in love with him. Completely."

Now the room was silent. Liam couldn't look around, didn't want to see the looks of pity.

"I told him a secret once, and he took care of it so perfectly. He made me brave enough to share it here, now. The truth is, I was scared of everything real, of everything that could make me feel anything at all. TV was all I knew, both in my personal and professional life. Liam is the most real person I've ever known. And he made me *feel* everything." She gave a half laugh. "You should see him with his son." The laugh twisted into a sigh. "Liam lives in what some would call a fantasy, in a beach-side town full of wonderful people. Viewers will see us kiss. That was real. They'll see us jump from the pier. That was real, too—I wanted to do something crazy and big and frightening, and I wanted to do it with *him*."

The bar was silent.

Felicia looked straight into the camera. "Liam, I apologize for hurting you. I should have just stayed where I was, on the other side of the camera." Her hand went to her neck and touched the silver chain.

Liam knew that if he looked around every pair of eyeballs would be trained on him, not on the screen.

So he kept his own gaze up. It was good of her to apologize. To keep the part where he admitted he felt unlovable off the air was good of her. And for the network *not* to hurt his brothers with announcing what shits their parents were was pretty damn decent.

God.

Maybe it hadn't actually been that big a deal.

Felicia had kept his fear of abandonment and his family troubles off air. And she'd gone one step further—airing her own deepest secret for the whole nation to hear. It was a message to him, for him, that said she had taken care of his trust. She hadn't betrayed him.

Shit.

Big-screen Felicia fiddled with the collar of her black shirt. "But Liam, I wish you would have answered my calls. Even once."

He felt his brothers turn to face him, but he didn't take his eyes off the screen.

"I'm in love with you. But you abandoned me."

He lost his breath. Each word was a strike, a blow.

"Maybe we could have worked it out. Now

we'll never know." She shrugged, tears shining in her eyes. "You shouldn't have left me like that."

She didn't say it. She didn't tell the whole nation that *he* was the one terrified of being left behind.

It was a message just for him.

He'd become the person he'd never wanted to be.

Holy shit.

Liam left the bar at a run.

<h1 style="text-align:center">THIRTY-SEVEN</h1>

As the show ended and as the screen rolled to the credits, Felicia ran out of the treehouse. The door locked automatically behind her, but that was okay—her key was around her neck. She'd never be locked out again.

Liam had made sure of that.

Goddamn him.

It wasn't until she was halfway down the driveway, stumbling in the dark, that she realized she was headed toward town.

Toward him.

A few nights before, Felicia had mapped the road to town on her phone while lying in her new bed, listening to the redwood creak just feet away from her head. The Golden Spike was only a little more than a mile, twenty, twenty-five minutes on foot.

Her flip flops slapped at the dust, and a rock poked her heel.

Maybe by the time she hit the town's street lights, she would come to her senses. She knew she wouldn't make it all the way to the Golden Spike. Adele Darling had invited her to watch the show with the rest of town: *You could meet everyone in one fell swoop.*

Felicia had been grateful, but had turned her down, preferring to watch the show alone and imagine the town's reaction in her own mind.

She could imagine it, frame by rapid frame.

Everyone would yell when they saw the Ballard Brothers on screen for the first time.

They'd hoot when Liam and Felicia kissed.

They'd applaud and clap him on the back when she apologized to him in her diary cam.

Then, probably, they'd be pissed when she said on camera that he'd abandoned her, but goddamn it, that was as true as the fact that she was sorry she'd hurt him.

He should have called her back, or emailed her, or at least texted her. Just once.

Instead, he'd ghosted.

And in doing so, he'd broken her already pulverized heart in the process.

Felicia tripped over a fallen branch and turned on her cell phone's flashlight. She'd walk a little way farther but *not* all the way to town. She'd just get some of this excess energy out of her legs, her body.

God*damn* him.

A low rumble of a motor got louder. Closer.

A MOTORCYCLE? Was that what that light was? Liam squinted to get a better view of the bright light shining at him.

It didn't act the way a motorcycle's headlight in the distance would. It was more bouncy, the light thinner.

Maybe a bicycle? But who the hell was riding a bike out here in the dark?

He couldn't figure out how far away the light was until suddenly he was almost on top of it.

On top of her. Felicia's face gleamed bright in his headlights.

He hit the brakes so hard the whole truck skidded.

Jesus.

He'd almost hit her. He fumbled for the door handle, unsure if his heart was going to start beating again on its own or if he'd have to fall down in front of her and hope she pitied him enough to perform CPR.

"What the *hell* are you doing?" Her voice was high, on the edge of a scream.

"What are *you* doing?" His hands tingled so hard they hurt.

"You almost hit me!"

"*I almost hit you!*"

Felicia stood in the headlight's glare, dust from the road rising up around both of them. She was glaring at him so hard she might be able to burn holes through him. Except for the clicking of the engine as it cooled, the road was silent.

"Who wears black to go on a nighttime hike?" Liam's voice was a roar, and that wasn't fair. It wasn't her fault. He'd been going too fast. But he was angry, goddammit, for reasons he didn't dare name. Not yet.

"Someone who didn't plan on leaving the house! And who the hell drives that fast down country roads and doesn't slow down when he sees a light?"

Liam stuck his hand in his pockets, willing his heart to stop racing. "We could play this game all night, or you could tell me where you were headed."

"*For a walk.*"

"In the dark."

"I had a light." She held up her cell phone like she might chuck it at him.

"Wearing flip flops."

She looked down at her feet. "Well..."

"You watched the show."

She scowled harder at him. "So?"

"So you were coming to find me."

"*So?*"

Liam wanted to bellow, to laugh, to cry, to run, but all he did was stand in place on the dusty road. It took every ounce of his courage he'd ever possessed to say, "So I was coming to find you, too."

Felicia clutched the key at her neck. Her eyes were wide, and only now did he notice they were full of tears. "You're *late*."

HE WAS *SO* LATE. If she weren't wearing sandals, she'd kick something—his tires, his shins, maybe. "I did *everything* except take out a singing telegram to apologize to you."

"I know." Liam's arms hung loosely at his sides.

"And you *ignored* me."

"I know."

Dust still rose, but slower now. Liam was silhouetted in the truck's headlights, and she couldn't see his face clearly. "You did exactly what you hate other people to do—you left. Except it was worse. I saw you in town twice."

"Wait, what? I didn't see you."

"Well, I *hid.*"

His voice was low. "You what?"

Felicia bit her bottom lip so hard she tasted blood. Then she admitted, "I ran behind the post office once, and the other time I dove into the storeroom at the Golden Spike." Both times, she'd wanted to do the opposite—to run to him. But both times, she chickened out. The only time she'd found the nerve to go to his house, Timbo had looked at her with something like pity in his eyes. *He's not here. You want me to give him a message?*

She'd sent her own messages enough times to know he wasn't interested in returning them.

His hands turned, opening toward her, then pulling back. "Felicia—"

"You should have answered."

"I know."

Why did he keep *saying* that? She crossed her arms. "Why didn't you, then?"

"Licking my wounds, I guess."

"Why now?" But she knew. He'd seen the show. "You want to tell me I'm wrong. You want to tell me you didn't abandon anyone, ever, and that I shouldn't have said that, and that you're pissed off, and buddy, I hear you. I'm pissed off, too—"

Liam stepped forward. "I'm going to kiss you."

Felicia threw her head back and groaned. "What is *wrong* with you?"

"I'm just warning you. I don't want you to run away when I do it." He took another step. He was only an arm's length away now. "You've already admitted you run away from me sometimes."

Her heart raced and her fingers trembled. "I admitted on national television I was in love with you. Yes, I would like to run away to Antigua. Alone. As soon as possible. The *last* thing I want is you kissing me." It was the biggest lie she'd ever told.

"Before I kiss you, though, I'm going to apologize. I'm so sorry. You're right. I was in the wrong."

Felicia dug her fingernails into her arm. "What?"

"Oh, and the most important part. I love you, too."

Felicia sat.

Right in the dirt.

Her legs just wouldn't hold her up and she didn't have that much faith in her spine either, come to that.

Liam was still backlit so she stared at his knees. "Run that by me one more time?"

He crouched in front of her. "I'm completely, totally in love with you."

Felicia's face felt hot, but her chest felt cold. "I don't know—what do we *do* about that?"

"I kiss the hell out of you."

She wanted that—god, she wanted that. But—"What about after that, though?"

"I have no idea."

Dust rose in her nose, and she rubbed it. "Me neither."

"Are you staying? In Darling Bay?"

"I have a house here, you might have heard."

Liam shook his head. "I have one of those, too. But it doesn't feel like home anymore, honestly."

She could barely breathe around the lump in her throat. "Why not?"

"Because you're not there."

"Home," she whispered.

Liam reached forward and touched the key at her neck. "Is here."

He kissed her, hard and long, his hands tangling in her hair. He murmured words she couldn't understand, words she'd have time to figure out later. All the time in the world.

And Felicia kissed him back, hearing, as she did, the sound of her latchkey heart opening. For good.

EPILOGUE

What he'd built for her was silly, Liam knew it.

But silliness didn't seem to bother Felicia.

"Close your eyes."

Felicia laughed. "You've said that like five times, and I have a blindfold on. If I close them any harder, I'll be looking out my ears."

He led her forward, past the bed. "Don't trip on the rug."

"I love this rug." Felicia's bare feet moved slowly over it. "I don't know if I've mentioned that."

Liam smiled. "You might have. Once or twice." Felicia had made the rug herself. She'd taken a class in town with Talia Moorhead, and had braided it together out of an antique quilt top too shredded to be repaired. She'd spent about a week marveling at its beauty and even now only let him stand on it if he was barefoot.

"Okay. Up the ladder."

"Up to the treehouse blindfolded? Is this some kinky new thing?"

"It wasn't going to be, but I can rectify that if you want me to."

She grinned and put her hands on the middle rungs, lifting her foot to the bottom one. "What if I fall?"

"I'll catch you."

Her smile softened. "You always do."

Liam got more anxious. He was building this up too much. She might hate it. What if he'd over-stepped?

"Up! Going up!" she announced.

Liam followed the excellent view of Felicia's jeans-clad ass, just steps behind her. "When you reach the platform—yeah, you're almost there, swing yourself sideways, and sit with your feet hanging off."

She laughed, the sound of it happy and bright. "I *really* hope I don't fall."

If she actually did—and he prayed she wouldn't —he'd learn how to fly in time to catch her. He didn't know how, but he would do it.

"I love you," he said, sliding onto the platform next to her. He didn't get tired of saying it. Six months in, and the words meant more every damn time.

"I love you, too." Her hand went out, open, waiting for him to take it. She trusted him.

And god, the feeling of that was like sunlight after rain. He took her hand.

"Now what?" Her legs swung gently.

"Now you take off your blindfold."

"Aw. I was just kind of getting used to it." But she pulled it off and looked at him.

She looked at *him*. She didn't look around to see what he'd done—her eyes went first to Liam.

He kissed her.

She kissed him back.

Life was pretty goddammed perfect, and she hadn't even seen what he'd done up here yet.

Felicia pulled away. "Okay. Now I look."

She swiveled her head.

Then she gasped. She covered her mouth with her hand. "Oh. Liam."

It was a simple build. A bench, fixed to the platform itself, facing the view of the valley and the far-off rise that led to the ocean. Above it hung an umbrella-like awning, affixed to the tree itself.

"It opens and closes, in case you just want to look straight up. Now you can sit and read up here. In the sun or the rain."

"Liam."

"Do you like it?"

Silently, she nodded. She stood and sat on the bench, touching the top gingerly with her fingertips. "It's just big enough for two."

"Exactly big enough."

"It's...so perfect." Felicia ran her hands along the top of the bench, along the side bevel.

Liam shook his head. "It's crooked. There might be splinters even though I did my best to get rid of them."

Her eyes warmed him. "You didn't get Aidan or Jake to help you."

"Uh-uh."

"Timbo?"

"He might have helped a *little* bit. But I swear I'm better than he is with a hammer. Mostly."

The breeze shook the last gift, the one that hung from a simple hook, and Felicia laughed in what sounded like joy. "A wind chime! And is it...it's made of *keys*."

She touched them and they clunked companionably.

Liam felt like apologizing for them. "It's not the expensive, beautiful kind of wind chime. Not in tune or anything. Kind of tone-deaf, actually."

"It's perfect. Where are the keys from?"

It was the right question, and one he'd known she'd ask. "From a box at the antique shop. I picked through each key until I found the really worn ones. Look, they've all been handled thousands of times by people who loved their homes."

She kissed him hard, and then she said, "Move in."

Liam jumped, his heart in freefall. "What?"

"What if you and Timbo moved in? With me?"

"You mean live in sin?"

She clapped. "I *love* sin."

Liam let a breath fill his body. In. Out. Then, "Well, ma'am, what if it wasn't in sin?"

"I'm confused. Are we going to church now or something?"

He reached in his pocket. This wasn't the way he'd planned, not exactly. He'd thought he'd show her what he'd done to the treehouse, and next week, on her birthday, he'd ask her to marry him. But the ring was in his pocket, and the sunlight coming through the leaves was dappling her face with gold, and he couldn't take it anymore.

He held it out. "Another key."

"*What?*"

Liam pointed out how it was bent and formed, an old skeleton key that had been shaped into a ring. "See? It's an actual key."

Felicia was pale. "Is this—What does this key open?"

"Me. It opens me. You do that. Damn it, that

makes me sound like a beer bottle. I meant to—" Liam slid off the bench and onto one knee. "I had big plans. Skywriting or something. Dancing in the moonlight. I wasn't sure yet. But I can't wait, not one second longer. Felicia Turbinado, will you marry me?" His heart clunked harder than the keys in the breeze.

Felicia stayed silent. Her eyes were bigger than he'd ever see them. He could almost see himself reflected there, in the darkness of her corneas.

A sudden wind shook the boughs above, and a flurry of redwood needles skittered across the wooden platform. "Felicia? Darlin'?"

Felicia shook her head. "Yes! Of course, yes!"

Relief was thick as honey in his mouth as he kissed her. And it sweetened like molten sugar as she kissed him back, the heat getting higher, faster.

"Up here?" she grinned, tugging up his T-shirt. "To celebrate."

"No one around to see us but the squirrels."

"And this bench." Felicia raised an eyebrow. "We should probably see how strong it is."

"You really said yes? To me? You understood the question and all?"

"I did," Felicia said against his lips. "And I'm not going anywhere."

He felt himself grow harder. "Why did you hesitate?"

"Oh." Her cheeks flamed.

"What?"

"I was just...I was just feeling it. It felt so good, to hear you ask, that I thought I'd just think about it for a minute."

"Feels pretty good."

She laughed, and her eyes sparkled. Then she slid her hand inside the fly of his jeans. "I have to agree."

And there, at the top of the tree, Liam and Felicia made love with no one to hear the clunking of the wind chime and their cries of joy except two curious squirrels and one surprised passing hawk. The hawk examined the situation closely in two long drive-by swoops, and then flew higher up and away, searching for his own mate to settle with onto the limb of a great and sheltering tree. To settle into home.

The End

DEAR READER

Dear Reader,

I got the idea for this series in a strange but sweet place—at the foot of a hospital bed as my mother-in-law lay drowsing. While we rubbed her swollen feet, we watched the most soothing TV of all: HGTV. The Property Brothers were new to me, and I have to admit, I still find them a bit weird. I do NOT think Liam, Aidan, or Jake look like them, and I'm super glad they don't have their shellacked hair or giganto teeth.

But what I loved about them was their calm. Their big hands. The way they treated houses like THINGS YOU CAN TAKE APART. (As I type this, there are literally two men underneath my feet, putting in a new furnace. Yes, it does too get cold in California in the winter. It's 56 degrees in my office right now! You should see what I'm wearing—ALL THE LAYERS. Those HVAC men know approximately one million times more than I do about what to do with a screwdriver, and yeah. It's sexy.)

And I have to admit—I'm a Bachelor watcher. While my darling MIL dozed, I imagined the best case scenario: brothers who would date the woman who got to keep the house. Hot and sweet, my two favorite things.

I'm happy to say my MIL loved the idea, and her twin sister read her this book in the hospital (no, we CANNOT think about the sex scenes in this context. Nope, nope, nope).

And when she was done, my mother-in-law said in her sweet Texas drawl, "Where's the next one, honey? I need to read about Aidan." Well, Jeannie, this one's for you.

Love,

Rachael

PS - Turn the page to see what Aidan thinks of being part of this show. Jeannie, you were so right about him. ;)

Build it Strong, Book 2

BUILD IT STRONG

Aidan couldn't have been in a blacker mood if the earth had stopped rotating, leaving California's coast in perpetual darkness. He pulled up in front of the old Callahan house with a roar of tires, a spray of gravel, and an attitude that could strip paint.

The woman had chosen the *wrong* damn house.

And it was all Liam's fault.

A cameraperson waved jauntily from the porch, but Aidan ignored him.

He got out of his truck. When he strapped on his tool belt, his scowl was so deep it actually hurt his jaw.

His brother came out onto the porch. "Hurry

up!" Liam slapped at his watch. "You're twenty minutes late."

Who cared? Aidan sure didn't. "The Golden Spike was crowded."

"And you couldn't get your coffee to go just *once*."

Aidan shook his head. "I like to sit at the counter in the morning. You know that."

"I know you jawjack with the old guys like you're seventy."

"Is she here?"

"Tuesday?"

"Whatever the hell her dumb day-of-the-week name is."

Liam folded his arms over his fancy pinstriped shirt that probably cost a hell of lot more than Aidan's three-for-ten-dollars T-shirt had. "You sure woke up with your pants on cranky."

Cranky? Understatement of the century. Aidan was mad as hell. "Yeah?"

"Seriously, you have to keep that attitude off camera."

Aidan rested his hand on his favorite hammer as if he were a sheriff with his hand on his holster. "It'll make the show spicier, don't you think?"

"No, I think it'll make us look like a bunch of country-yokel jackasses."

"Whatever. Let's just get the filming over with."

Liam blocked Aidan from entering the house with his body. "I'm not kidding. Pull it together. I don't care how you feel about this house. It's hers now."

That was the whole goddamn problem. This house—this old, perfect, wonderful, gorgeous beast of a house—belonged to someone who wasn't Aidan. To a woman who was coming in from the outside. "*I* was going to buy it. You know I was."

Liam winced. "And I wanted you to. But your bid wasn't accepted."

"You could have made sure it was."

"You would have had to outbid her big time."

Aidan had only had enough in savings for a small down payment. If he'd sold his condo in time, he could have probably outbid her. "Yeah, well, I would have needed you to sell my condo for me."

Liam bristled. "*You* would have needed to make that decision about two months earlier."

"I'm supposed to know the future?"

"Besides, the seller chose *her*."

Aidan's jaw tightened. "The seller is LouAnn Callahan's ungrateful cousin who never even came to town to look at the place, and you're the broker. You should have pulled some strings. It was my dream." The words felt like gravel in his throat. He shouldn't have to say this to his brother. Liam *knew*.

"I know. Does it help that you still get to work on it?"

"Seriously?" An outsider would tell him what kind of crappy tiles she wanted. He'd have to build an in-house sauna or something else just as ridiculous for her. It would all happen on film, with the television cameras rolling. She'd be the customer and she'd have to be right. About everything. Then he and his brothers would hand over her key at the end of this episode of *On the Market*. He'd never have another chance at owning the place he'd loved since he was ten.

From the entryway, the cameraperson named Anna called, "Hey guys, the light is coming into the kitchen perfectly. Let's catch this."

"We're coming," Liam said over his shoulder. Then he said to Aidan, "Get a grip. I mean it."

Aidan rubbed a hand over his mouth. He tried on a half-smile, but it didn't fit his face.

Liam shook his head. "You look like you're about to chew off someone's leg."

"It's going to be yours, if you don't get out of my way."

Inside, it was chaos. The living room was full of light poles aimed toward the group standing in the dining room. Extension cords coiled over every inch of floor.

"Powder, sir?" A kid who couldn't have been more than nineteen tried to wave a brush in his face, but she ran away when Aidan scowled.

A complete stranger tugged at Aidan's T-shirt and adjusted his tool belt while another person stuck a mic pack into the back of Aidan's pants. "I feel violated," he said, but no one was paying the slightest bit of attention to him.

"Rolling," someone yelled.

Liam waved him into the kitchen. "Aidan, I want you to meet our client. This is Tuesday Willis."

The woman was medium height with a medium build. She had medium brown hair that was medium length and the medium brown eyes to match. She wore cat-eye black glasses that were probably in fashion but which really served to make her look like a librarian. There was nothing remarkable about her except the fact that she'd stolen Aidan's house right out from underneath him. She might have been tolerably pretty if Aidan hadn't despised her so much already. But hell, the more he hated her, the less chance she'd choose him to date during the renovation. If Aidan did his job right, there was a one-hundred percent chance she would choose Jake as her on-screen date-night target.

She smiled.

Aidan didn't.

Her handshake was firm, but clammy.

Liam said, "Tuesday, this is my brother Aidan. He'll be the work foreman, the one in charge of the renovation. That's Jake over there."

Jake, the idiot, waved cheerfully. Yeah, he wasn't losing his dream today. Tuesday smiled back.

Liam went on, "I thought we could get a head start on what you might be thinking of doing with this place."

"Well, I—"

Aidan cut her off. "And what *is* that?" He could practically feel the camera zooming in on his face. Sixteen million people would watch him be a son of a bitch on television, but he didn't care.

"Sorry?"

"What is it that you want to do with this place, exactly- ?"

Tuesday glanced at Liam. "Should we just jump into that?"

Liam nodded. "Sure. Why don't you walk us through a couple of rooms and tell us your vision for the place."

"Okay, then." With her forefinger, she pushed up her glasses. Her nails were painted, predictably, medium pink. "Well, I guess I was thinking—"

"What are you going to do with the wood?" Aidan thumped the frame of the door that led into the kitchen. It was old Doug fir, and while it was scratched and dinged, it was perfection itself.

"Um. Paint it? I was thinking yellow walls with white trim?" She looked up at the dark beams that soared overhead. "Wouldn't that be pretty?"

She'd just failed.

"No." Aidan brushed past her, ignoring the fact that her face had fallen. He led the way into the kitchen. "What about in here? What's your idea of fixing this up?"

Tuesday had rallied and was smiling at the camera. Obviously, they hadn't told her that she wasn't *supposed* to look at the cameras, that she was supposed to talk just to the other people as if there wasn't an entire crew hanging on their every word. "Well, I love this old sink."

She was right about that. A deep farmhouse ceramic sink, it was perfect, set deep and low in the old butcher-block countertops.

Aidan waited.

"But I was thinking of marble countertops. You know?"

There it was. No surprises here. Turning his dream home into a hipster Pinterest house was going to be the worst gig in the history of Aidan's construction career. "Let me guess. You're looking for more of an open plan."

She smiled, her face lighting up. Behind those

glasses, her eyes sparkled. For one moment, Aidan felt the tiniest bit guilty about growling at her.

Then she said, "Exactly. If the dining room led into—"

"Yeah. I get it. Hang on." He stalked past the crew, out the living room, and to his truck. The cool, damp outside air was welcome against his heated face. He pulled out his biggest sledgehammer and stormed back inside, holding it like a baseball bat.

"Aidan." Liam's voice was a warning.

"No, I get it. I see our client's vision. I know how this is going to work. Let's get this show on the road."

Ignoring the roar in his own head, Aidan pulled on a pair of safety goggles. "You might want to stand back," he said to Tuesday.

"Wait, what?"

He swung the sledgehammer back with all the force of his body, slamming it through the wall that stood between the living room and dining room. Plaster rained down, the lathe behind it snapping like firewood. "There we go. A good start!"

Tuesday Willis stepped forward. She put one hand firmly on his chest, and with her other, took away his sledgehammer, hefting it as if it were a lightweight rubber mallet. She looked directly into his eyes, and Aidan felt a thud in his torso that he didn't see coming.

Enunciating clearly, Tuesday said, "That's a load-bearing wall, you *idiot*."

KEEP READING NOW!

Build it Strong, Book 2

ABOUT RACHAEL

Rachael Herron is the internationally best-selling author of more than twenty books, including thriller (under R.H. Herron), mainstream fiction, feminist romance, memoir, and nonfiction about writing. She received her MFA in writing from Mills College, Oakland, and she teaches writing extension workshops at both UC Berkeley and Stanford. She is a proud member of the NaNoWriMo Writer's Board. She's a New Zealand citizen as well as an American.

She'd love to hear from you!
Facebook | Twitter | Blog | Patreon